THE LOST COLLEGE
AND
OTHER OXFORD STORIES

THE LOST COLLEGE
AND
OTHER OXFORD STORIES

OxPens

OxPens
Copyright © Contributors 2008

First published in Great Britain 2008 by OxPens in conjunction with WritersPrintShop

ISBN: 1904623123

CONTENTS

Also from Oxpens

The Sixpenny Debt

&

other **Oxford** stories

"A wonderful collection for everyone who loves this beautiful city and its countryside." Katie Fforde

Valerie Petts

THE SIXPENNY DEBT AND
OTHER OXFORD STORIES
ISBN 1904623468

FOREWORD

Over the years many wannabee writers have asked me to make some judgement upon their (occasionally, alas, very lengthy) literary efforts. Such a process, for me, has too often been a disappointing and dispiriting affair, since grammatical and syntactical competence has not infrequently been of 'sub-primary' standards – a bit like American mortgages, perhaps.

What therefore surprised, indeed delighted me about the Oxford Writers' Group's Volume I was the high standard of technical expertise displayed therein; and – an even bigger surprise – was the regular display throughout the short stories of new-minted and entertaining ideas.

Volume II? Well, a common reference in the publishing world is the peril of 'the second-book hurdle', at which a good many runners in the Writers' Stakes have come to grief, some of them incurring a plenitude of penalty points. Not so here! Our talented writers have collectively cleared the hurdle with stylish assurance.

Fourteen of the two dozen or so Group members have submitted their stories, and they cover a splendidly wide range: from humour and satire to psychological insights; from history, old and new, to romance and reflection; and to add a dash of spice we find spookery and science fiction too.

Short-story writing is a difficult art, and it is a remarkable achievement of these writers that after finishing one tale in their anthology, the reader – believe me – will be more than ready – eager, rather – to begin the next.

COLIN DEXTER

AFTERMATH

JANE STEMP

She was leaning on the parapet of Magdalen Bridge, apparently looking down at the river, both hands deep in the pockets of a greatcoat too big for her. He had been walking in the Botanic Gardens, for want of anything better to do on a Saturday afternoon, but there are only so many hours you can kill in a garden in winter. A woman wearing trousers was - slightly - more interesting.

'I heard the war had changed women's habits, but I didn't know it went as far as trousers.' He reached out and fingered the stone, crumbly with lichen.

'And did it change your manners,' she retorted, 'or are you always impertinent to strangers?'

'I beg your pardon. I don't suppose it did me any good, no. But if that's your brother's greatcoat, you look charming in it.'

'It was my cousin's. And I cut lunch with a tutor so that I could go to his funeral, if you must know.' She seemed to shrink inside the coat. 'This *bloody* influenza.'

There was nothing he could think of to say: he tilted his head slightly, trying to see her face beyond the curve of dark hair. 'I'm sorry. Very sorry.'

'It only takes the strongest. The best. *It's not fair*.' She turned and began to walk away towards the High Street.

'Doesn't it always? Why else would I still be here... don't go,' he said, and was surprised to see her stop and turn back.

'Why not?' she asked.

'You'll be in trouble, to start with. Out unchaperoned.' He took a few steps towards her.

1

She began to laugh, a low, bitter noise hardly to be heard as a carriage rattled by. 'I was in the base hospital at Rouen when they bombed it, I've washed parts of men my maiden aunts hardly dared think of, and I'm supposed to be in danger on the streets of Oxford!'

'I know; ridiculous,' he said. 'I've run messages back of the trenches hoping like hell that the star shells don't show me up, and I have to be back in college by ten past nine.'

'You too?' They stopped and looked at each other, face to face for the first time. 'Béthune,' she said. 'You came in after Béthune.' Her mouth twitched. 'You had *measles!*'

'I know. My mighty war.' He smiled. 'The perils of being billeted on a family.' He took off his hat. 'I thought it was you, when... when you spoke. The tall nurse who brought in rabbits for the pot. We used to wonder who shot them.'

'I did, as it happens. I'm a good shot. Some of us were brought up in the country.' She brushed her hair out of her eyes in a gesture he had last seen when she was scrubbing the floor by Captain Carrow's bed.

'Despite the maiden aunts,' he said.

'*By* the maiden aunts. I used to escape when I could.' She looked at him, laughter glinting in her eyes. 'Am I going to be in worse trouble if I go back alone, or if you come with me?'

He held out his hat. 'Put that on. It should pass muster as far as...?'

'The Woodstock Road, or until someone notices my heels. Thank you.' She crammed it on to her head, and tucked the ends of her hair up under it.

'Don't tell me you're a Home Student.'

'Do I look like one?' She looked at him again. She *was* tall; her eyes were almost at a level with his.

'No. You don't.' He adjusted the hat to the correct angle. 'That's better.'

'Then the honour of my college is safe, at least.'

They crossed Longwall and walked for a while in silence, past the Mitre, with the cold wind at their backs, and past the University Church. Suddenly he said, 'It doesn't seem real, you know. Being back. I used to hold on to this place, in my head, when it was all mud and noise out there. Now...' They crossed Turl Street and turned right, changing places so that he was on the outside of the pavement still.

'Now,' she said, '*it's* real enough. But we don't belong. We're like ghosts here, but still living. The freshers - they seem so shrill and silly. I can hardly bear it sometimes.' She glanced sideways into the window of a jeweller's shop.

'Young and innocent. Don't blame them. You've earned the right to be here if anyone has.' He shivered. 'Could we move on?'

'I'm sorry. You must be cold without your hat.' She moved as if to take his left arm, but remembered herself when he stepped forward.

'No. I dreamt about this street last night. That the paving stones were all thrown up, as if by shells, and underneath was - like No Man's Land. All bones and bits and - ' Though the wall was to his left, he leaned on it briefly with his right arm. 'I'm sorry. I should stop.'

'It sounds as if you've earned your place here too,' she said.

'What about the ones who didn't make it? Didn't they earn theirs?' He stood straight again, and walked off not waiting for her.

'Yes they did,' she said fiercely, half-running to catch up. 'Of *course* they did. And some thought they had it, like Jim, and then the influenza got them all the same. Is that fair?'

'Fair? No. The way of the world? Probably.' After a few minutes he asked, 'Do you remember them all? Jack LeStrange from the House, and the Canadians? That boy from the Naval Brigade, and Ned Carrow who got in such a rage when someone stole his precious souvenir Mauser?'

'I remember them,' she said. 'We all teased Captain Carrow dreadfully when it turned out the rifle wasn't missing after all.'

'Wasn't it? I don't remember that.'

She stopped in her tracks suddenly, as if startled, though it might have been to avoid the cyclist turning, un-signalling and un-belled, out of Broad Street. 'No - of course you wouldn't. It was after...'

'Oh. Yes.' His voice, which had been so animated, deadened suddenly. 'You know, my mamma always used to tell me, be careful what you ask for. You might get it.'

Broad Street was behind them, the blank corner of Balliol to their right as they turned northward into St Giles'. She said, gently, tentatively, 'I remember what you asked for.'

He laughed, tipping his head back and running his hand through the short, fair hair. 'I was desperate, wasn't I? I'm such a coward. Just a nice little Blighty one, enough to send me home discharged unfit for service.'

A few of last year's leaves still hung withered on the plane trees, or cracked under their feet. He kicked at them.

She bit her lip. 'You were running a high fever. You might not have meant it.'

'Oh, I meant it all right. And I got it, didn't I? Thanks to some German sniper and *his* fancy Mauser. I tell you, our boys really used to envy them that optical sight.' He shrugged. 'I suppose it was damn silly of me to go sight-seeing so near the lines.'

She said, in a strained voice, 'Probably. I think Matron was more upset by the fact that you disobeyed orders.'

'I dare say. She was a tartar. If she ever heard that my left hand's totally useless, she probably regards it as a judgment.' They walked on in silence until he said, 'We're almost up to the church. You'd better cross the road.'

'I had, hadn't I? The path by the south door is best.' They dropped into single file between the low walls, and crossed the Woodstock Road.

'Thank you for seeing me back,' she said. 'I must have taken you out of your way.'

'Not necessarily. Maybe I'll go for a walk,' he said lightly. 'Out to Port Meadow to read Housman, or something pathetically romantic like that.'

'Not much like Shropshire, is it?' she said. 'I'm from Church Stretton.' They passed the line of shops, and St Aloysius' church, primly drawn back from the road.

He stopped by the corner of the college, against the railings, and said, 'He *knows*, though, doesn't he? Old Housman? "That is the land of lost content." Or if he doesn't know, how come he says it for me?'

She finished the quotation for him. '"Those happy highways where I went / And cannot come again." But you are here again, after all.'

'Happy? Maybe.' He shook his head. 'Don't mind me. I'm... glad we met.' He looked sideways at her. 'So Ned Carrow's Mauser turned up after all?'

'Yes. A few days later. Where it was all along, hidden up in his bed-springs.' She handed his hat back to him and shook her hair loose. 'Thanks for the loan. I'll try to get in with someone else, or go round to Walton Street and climb through Cicely's window.'

'Take care,' he said. 'What's for dinner in hall tonight? Rabbit?'

Her laughter was unconvincing. 'If it is, I shan't eat it. Never again.'

He said, slowly, 'Do you still shoot?'

'Not any more.' She looked at him, a crease between her brows. 'Why do you ask?'

'No reason in the world.' He watched her for a moment, and then said, 'I could have wished the sniper had gone for the other hand. I'd been looking for a decent excuse to give my mamma for not using the right one, ever since I started school.' He stepped back as a cluster of students arrived and crowded round the wicket door. 'Here's your Trojan horse.'

She didn't lift her feet high enough, and stumbled at the threshold. 'You're left-handed?' she said.

'I was. That sniper did something my mamma never could.' He touched his hat to her. 'I won't shake hands, if you don't mind.' And he went on, northward, left hand in his pocket. For a while she watched him, and then began to cry silently, clinging to the edge of the door. Under her hands it was as smooth and worn as a rifle stock.

THE GARDENER'S TALE

ROSIE ORR

' ... Take the carrier bag for me, will you? An' don't swing it about, the contents is delicate...

'Eh? ...No, I can't say. You don't need to know, not yet. All will be revealed in the fullness. Should we be accosted en route to our objective by some ruddy student wantin' advice on growin' marijuana in 'is window box or one of them tourist groups demandin' to take your photograph on account of your quaintly rustic rake an' hoe – that Alan Titchmarsh's got a lot to answer for, if you ask me – say it's your lunch.

'...Take it you signed the secrecy wossit when you was approached?... Well don't never forget it. Come to a very sticky end if you let so much as an 'int slip about your Special Duties, you could. Be checkin' your brakes on your moped every time you nip down the Co-op, if you follow -me...

'Eh? ...Let's just say one of the gardeners up Christ Church recruited to a very similar position to your own found 'isself one over the eight one night in an 'ostelry near the coach station and was 'eard to make reference to a certain 'ush 'ush venue on the western perimeter of Christ Church grounds to the existence of which 'e 'ad been made privy. Well as 'eaven's me judge – come a bit closer, careful, mind me spade – *'e's never been seen from that day ter this.*

'...Keep on walkin' – an' act natural, trick is to look as if you're off to do a bit of prunin' or weedin'.

'Eh? ...Oh yes. Layin' of slug pellets'd be very acceptable... Turn left 'ere by the tennis courts. Not far now. Pay attention to the landmarks, cos next week you'll be on your own.

The Lost College and Other Oxford Stories

'...So. Rhododendron bushes on your left; where they give out you've got your laurel 'edge. Don't like the look of the rust on them railin's... Comin' to the compost 'eaps, now. Terrible smell. In fact wouldn't surprise me if they stashed the lad from Christ Church 'ere, *hurr hurr*... No need to look like that – only jokin'. Much more likely they sunk 'im in the lake up Worcester College wearin' concrete boots, if you ask me... Keep up, now, time's getting' on – down to mark out the cricket pitch this afternoon, ain't you? Won't do to be late, questions of an awkward nature could be asked.

'...Right. End of this gravel path you've got your leylandii, see? The Dean's idea, the leylandii was, which just goes to show the old bugger's not as gaga as 'e looks. Put anyone off, they would... Now. See them little grey stones? Mark a gap where you can squeeze through the foliage. That's it – keep shovin' your way through, I'm right be'ind you. Watch yourself on them branches, 'ave your eye out if you're not careful - lethal, they are. Oh yes, definitely got to 'and it to the Dean... What d'you mean, wossat? Drystone wall, innit... Why're we stoppin'? Cos be'ind this curtain affair of ivy an' cobwebs an' that there is – *tah dah*! A wooden door. Which, if you'll 'old me spade a mo – ta – I will now proceed, if I can get me key out of me pocket - blimey, ruddy thing weighs a ton, why it's got to be all fancy wrought iron an' that I do not know – to unlock. There. Squeaks somethin' shockin', don't it... Right. You'll find you got to give it a bit of a shove, wood's all swelled on account of the rain an' that... There. And it's... *Open Sesame!!*

'...Well don't just stand there gawpin' – get yourself inside so I can get that door closed again. An' shut your mouth, there's flies about, *hurr hurr*... So. 'Ere we are. Don't know what you was expectin', but I'll bet a pound to a pinch of porridge it weren't this, eh? Thought it were goin' to be all marble statues an' that, didn't you?

'...Right. Can see it's goin' to take a while for you to take it all in, an' we ain't got long, so bearin' in mind you'll be doin' this on your lonesome from next week reckon the best thing's for you to park yourself on that

8

plaster toadstool while I go about me duties. Right. Watch an' learn...

'...Basically all you got to do is keep things nice, check the batteries an' keep up the stocks of nosh an' pale ale an' that. Fuse box is be'ind the plastic vine 'ere, see? Spares an' replacements an' that – bulbs for the frosted fairy lights round the vine, similar for the pink rubber light-up lotuses on the water feature – stashed in a false compartment down the birdbath column over there near the barbie. Watch out for them plaster squirrels glued round the edge if you're 'avin' a rummage.

'...Oh, very lifelike, yes... Eh? Same as yer gran's but two of 'ers 'ave got their 'eads missin'?...Well she wants to do somethin' about 'er neighbour's cat, in my opinion... Movin' on. Cheese footballs an' twiglets inside the eezi-wipe life-size Venus de Milo; twiddle 'er left nipple an' 'er bum swings open like... so. Lovely job. 'Inges need a drop of WD-40 every once in a while - you'll find that down the birdbath an' all, ditto them little pots of modellin' paints for touchin' up the spots on the toadstools. Right. Fuel brickettes an' that for the barbie stashed in a B&Q carton under the swing recliner with orange and lime green striped canopy under them plastic palms, Mexican chicken wings an' 'amburgers an' that in a freezer jobbie under the deckin'.

'Eh? The *only* one? Lor' bless you, most of the colleges 'ave got somethin' similar 'idden away in their grounds. Me predecessor 'ad a colleague, 'ead gardener up St – well, best not say where, exactly, then you can't give nothin' away should anythin' untoward befall... Anyway, the aforementioned establishment not only 'ad a little retreat similar to this secreted up the scrub where the college grounds run down to the Isis – come Christmas, said little retreat 'ad to be transformed into a bleedin' Winter Wonderland, if you please.

'...You may well ask. Fake snow all over the astroturf, blow-up laughin' Father Christmas the size of an 'ouse with flashin' light-up eyes an' optional 'o-'o-'o, 'erd of life-size plastic reindeer with noddin' 'eads, plastic icicles danglin' everywhere. Amount of extra work involved must 'ave been shockin' – all that blowin' up an' constant battery changin'... Word ever reaches 'Igh Table 'ere, mark my words, it'll be only a matter of time before the Argos Christmas catalogue finds itself bein' passed round the Senior Common Room, an'... well, it don't do to think.

'...Nearly time we was off. Just got to give the gilt-effect Versailles-style table an' matchin' chairs for Alfresco Entertainin' a bit of a wipe – they're devils, them pigeons are – an' check the lights an' water features an' that. There... all done. Now. Controls is by the door, be'ind this panel concealed by artificial webbin' with Arachnid Effect. Let's see - water feature effect: GO.

'...Very impressive, yes, the way the waves make them lotuses bob up an' down... Right, next. Fairy lights round plastic grape vine: GO.

'...Lovely job. An' don't forget to check the angle of the dangle from time to time – bulbs come into contact wiv them plastic leaves, you can only imagine the conflagration that would result. Now, automatic bird song: GO.

'...Oops. Double speed, my mistake... There, that's better.

'...Right. Now normally you just come in twice a week in your lunch break an' do the necessary as instructed. 'Owever, if there's any special instructions or they've 'ad a bit of a whip round cos one of 'em's 'ad some 'alf-baked research published or invented some crackpot new theory or other an' they want to place an order for a new item to commemorate same they'll leave the Argos catalogue or similar – remember the carrier I give you to carry from 'Omebase? – in the ornamental wheelbarrer, with used notes stuffed in an envelope. Can't be traced back, see? Same with your pay. Cash in a Pringles tube be'ind the rockery first Friday of the month. Supplement your basic wage very nicely, that will.

'...Speakin' of new items, if you'll 'and me the aforesaid carrier... Ta. Whistlin' Gnome, they ordered 'im last week – yer prob'ly seen in the *Oxford Mail*, some foreign geezer bunged College a ton of money to fix somethin' or other, reckon they decided to celebrate... *Tah dah!!* See?

Bell on 'is little cap tinkles if you shake 'im. Love this, the dons will. An' the Dean'll wet 'isself. As for the Master, 'e'll prob'ly 'ave an 'eart attack 'e'll be so excited – reckon 'e's close to carkin' it anyway, if 'is colour's anything to go by. Sort of plum. Drop too much port after 'e's 'ad 'is tea up 'Igh Table, if you ask me... So, let's see. Where to put 'im...

'...Under them red 'ot pokers? Could do... could do... Oh yes. Very nice, you definitely got an eye – goin' to do very well in your new position I should say, very well indeed. Right. Any questions before we go?

'...Why? ...*Why*? Because between you an' me an' Mr Gnome there in 'is little spotted shorts, what you got to grasp is this: underneath them robes wiv the bits of fur and tassles an' that you see 'em mincin' about in – underneath all the 'igh falutin' chat in posh voices as in – let's see, now: *pass the Champagne an' caviar if you please Vice-Chancellor an' by the way I do believe I come up wiv an astonishin' new theory of the universe while I was 'avin' a bit of a ponder in me bath this mornin'* – your average academic is not overburdened with the old grey matter.

'...I know. Come as a bit of a shock to me, too, when I clocked it. Thing is, they got to keep up a front, see. People ever realised all your dons an' profs an' tutors an' that was good for was poncin' about in dressin'-up clothes an' talkin' weird they'd be down the Labour sooner than you can say Che Guevara, an' the College of Further Ed would be stagin' a coup quicker than a rat up a drainpipe.

'...Still, you got to feel sorry for 'em. Must be a terrible strain, all that jabberin' an' mincin' – no wonder the poor buggers need somewhere they can relax an' be their natural selves every Saturday night. Sad, really. Anyway, now I'm retirin' it's up to you to keep things shipshape... Right. Electrics off, check. Panel door closed, check. Artificial webbin' wiv Arachnid Effect in place, check. Ensure no instructions been left in ornamental wheelbarrer, check. Collect garden implements, check. Right, you carry 'em, I'll lock up.

'...There. I'll let you 'ave the key – this little lot's all yours, now – and off we go. Watch yourself on them leylandii branches... Speakin' of camouflage, I 'ear from a source which must remain nameless Balliol's plannin' to plant a load of – *Blimey!* That the time? Gotta roll the Master's bleedin' croquet lawn before I knock off – then I'm off to celebrate me comin' freedom... By the way, do with cuttin' back, that laurel could – that railin's lookin' very shaky.

'Eh? Takin' the wife up Garsington, new production of *Il Re Pastore*. Mozart. Very interestin' little piece, one of 'is early works – wrote it for one of Empress Maria's sons who was up Salzburg for a quick butcher's, apparently. Your stereotypical Arcadian idyll, basically – lot of mistaken identity an' trans-class dressin' an' that. Can't compare *Pastore* to 'is later operas, of course – 'ave to say it's more of a serenata, in point of fact – but if you concentrate you can spot the seeds of *Cosi* and *Don G* an' that in a couple of arias – *L'amero, saro costante,* for instance. Got a lovely sustained violin obbligato, 'as *L'amero*. Gets me every time.

'...Right. Tennis courts is where we part company – *nota bene* there's a trainee fiddlin' about with the 'erbacious borders over there by the statue an' what looks 'orribly like a bleedin' Special Tour wavin' their camcorders about near the chapel, so act casual an' don't look back. Final word of advice: don't ever forget what I told you about that poor bugger from Christ Church...

'Eh?... Could be, could be – or the crypt up Trinity springs to mind, could 'ave stuffed 'im down an empty beer barrel. Or stashed 'im be'ind the organ loft up Wadham, quite possibly...

'...Oh, very 'ard cheese, yes. Way I see it, the aforementioned imbibed a coupla jars too many down the Elm Tree up Cowley Road one night, got a bit cocky, dropped an 'int or two to impress – an' *word got back*. Savage lot them academics are, under them fancy robes an' that. Take it as a warning, if I was you... Anyway, time I was off. Remember, *schtum's the word,* an' best of luck in your Special Duties.'

THROUGH A GLASS, DARKLY

GINA CLAYE

It had been a long time, thought Isobel as she gazed upwards at the stained glass window. Memories rose unbidden and her throat tightened.

'I can tell you the answer,' said a voice behind her.

Isobel turned round, startled.

'I've bought the guide book,' said the woman. 'Jonas' cloak is the only part made of stained glass; the rest is painted.'

'Oh... thanks.'

'Do you want to borrow my biro to fill it in?' she asked, pointing to the quiz sheet in Isobel's hands.

'No, it's OK thanks. I've got my own.' She must be polite, she reminded herself. This woman was only trying to be friendly.

'The rest have split up into twos and threes. Shall we go around together? Two heads are better than one when you're doing a quiz.'

'That... that's an idea, but I need the loo,' improvised Isobel. 'It'll probably take some time to find one. Don't wait for me; you might lose precious time.'

'Righty-ho,' said the woman. 'I'll catch the others up over there. Good luck.'

Isobel watched her receding back with relief, then, catching sight of an approaching group of tourists, obviously intent on seeing as much of Christ Church Cathedral as they could, made her way to the other side. Here it was peaceful, for the moment anyway. She sank gratefully on to a chair. How on earth had she got herself into this situation? But she knew only too well. She had been badgered into it by Sue.

'Isobel, you've been on your own for more than four years now. It's time you gave yourself a chance to meet someone new.'

'I meet people every day in my job.'

'As a doctor's receptionist? All the men you meet are married or ill, or both. You need an interesting hobby.'

'I've got a hobby.'

'Creative embroidery! How many men do you meet when you go off for a weekend of creative embroidery?'

'Well, none actually,' sighed Isobel.

'There you are. Just a whole lot of women, and however interesting they may be, they're not men. What you need to do is join a singles' group or go off on a singles' weekend.'

'I'll think about it,' said Isobel.

'No, do it. Look, I came across this ad in the paper.'

Isobel took the cutting and read it with some amusement. 'Make new friends, perhaps meet that special someone; join us on a singles' weekend and get to know Oxford.'

'Go on,' urged Sue, 'there's nothing to lose. You'll have a bit of fun, meet loads of men and wander round beautiful ancient buildings into the bargain.'

Well, thought Isobel, that was the idea anyway, and she had needed to get away, but it had soon become obvious at dinner last night that the majority on the weekend were women, and the handful of men they'd recruited were very unprepossessing.

She closed her eyes and let the peace of the ancient building soak into her. It was looking at the window without him that had caught her unawares, the sudden feeling of loss all over again. She could feel the tears starting and jerked her head defiantly. This may be the place but it definitely wasn't the time. She must pull herself together; she couldn't fall to pieces now. She needed something to distract her, however trivial. The quiz. She stood up, glared at the sheet in her hand, and picked a question at random.

"Off with his head! Who had his head removed?" Mm... perhaps something to do with *Alice in Wonderland*? She knew Lewis Carroll, the author, had been a don here at Christ Church.

'Can I help you? I used to be a guide here.' The man's voice startled her. 'I overheard you,' he smiled.

Isobel blinked back her tears. She hadn't realised she'd read it aloud.

'No, it's nothing to do with *Alice in Wonderland*,' he continued. 'It's over here. Come and see.'

He led her to a side chapel.

'Look at the window, at the centre panel up there.' Recovering herself, Isobel did so. It showed a man kneeling between what looked like a monk and four men with swords raised.

'The figure kneeling is Thomas Becket, Archbishop of Canterbury, murdered by King Henry II's knights. He was made a saint but during the Reformation he was condemned as a traitor and rebel and all images of him in the country were ordered to be destroyed.'

'But he's perfect apart from his head.'

'Yes - the church authorities managed to get away with just destroying his head.'

'It's a beautiful window,' said Isobel.

'The earliest in the cathedral; the glass is 1320. Stay and feast your eyes on it. I'm sorry I can't stay, but I help out here now and again and I've promised to lend a hand moving a stack of chairs.'

'Thank you,' said Isobel. 'I'm really grateful.' Thank goodness he hadn't seemed to notice she'd been crying.

I suppose, she thought slowly, I must look at stained glass windows for both of us now. It's up to me. She wondered, as she gazed up, about the men who had pieced the coloured glass together, craftsmen who had lived hundreds of years ago and who had left part of themselves in this beautiful work of art. What had Guy left to posterity? Two daughters, one just finished university, the other just starting. They were undoubtedly his most important legacy, and hers. But at least she still had a future to do something with.

She pulled herself up with a jerk. This wouldn't do. The elderly couple who had just gone past had given her a strange look. She felt vulnerable, uncertain of herself, and took refuge once again in the quiz. After all, she thought, as she looked down the list of questions, she might as well try to get something out of the weekend.

"Where are the sleeping pigs?" Right. Where did one find sleeping pigs in a cathedral; perhaps carved pew ends? There were marvellous ones in Cornwall; some of them quite pagan. She looked around; there were chairs here in the side chapel, not pews. Choir stalls, she'd go and look at the choir stalls. She crossed the aisle and turned into the chancel, and nearly bumped into a small group coming her way.

'Hello, have you got many answers?' It was that woman again.

'No,' she admitted. 'I'm looking for sleeping pigs.'

'Over there,' said the woman, pointing to the other side of the cathedral. 'We've got all the ones in here and we're off to the Dining Hall now. By the way, have you read the extra question at the end? There's a bottle of Champagne for anyone who manages to answer it, but how they expect us to get it, I really don't know. Just listen. "Who is the friend quoted in the last Harry Potter book?" I ask you,' she exploded, 'who in their right mind has bothered to read that childish fantasy?'

Isobel didn't answer. She'd read all the Harry Potter books and the last one quite recently. She'd thought it excellent and had cried her way through the last fifty pages. Fantasy it may be, but it was also a story of loss. She read the question again. "Who is the friend quoted in the last Harry Potter book?" Harry Potter had loads of friends; she couldn't single one out. And it must be something to do with Christ Church. She gave it up. She obviously wouldn't be drinking Champagne that evening.

Did she really want to find the sleeping pigs? A faint curiosity coupled with the fact that she was now surrounded by tourists again made her head for the less populated side of the cathedral. She picked her way through the choir stalls past an altar of black wood, and found herself standing alone in a side chapel.

The window in front of her was a riot of colour, scenes from the life of someone - a woman, perhaps a saint? She caught her breath. The interweaving of deep blues, reds, gold, the sheer movement, surely she could capture this, create in fabric and embroidery part of this swirl of story. Her brain raced and her fingers itched for her sketch book. In her mind she could see the silks, cottons and velvets, overlaid in places with net and stitchery that would bring it to life. She didn't have her sketch book but she had the back of her quiz sheet and a biro. Completely absorbed, unaware of time or people passing, she worked with swift strokes, capturing her ideas.

There, that would have to do. Blast, she'd dropped the biro. She bent down to retrieve it and as she straightened up saw the man who had shown her the Becket window coming towards her.

'I see you've found the Saint Frideswide window,' he said. 'Do you know the story?'

'No,' said Isobel. 'Saint Frideswide?'

'She's the patron saint of Oxford. According to legend she was the daughter of the King of Oxford, who founded a monastery for her.'

'She was a nun.'

'Yes, but it didn't stop the King of Leicester wanting to marry her and pursuing her. There she's fleeing Oxford, and down the bottom she's hiding in a pig sty.'

'Are the pigs asleep?' asked Isobel.

'They are in the next panel, asleep in the wood; you can see her rowing past them up the River Thames. There she's healing the sick, and can you see that red bolt of lightning? That's the King being struck blind.'

'It's almost like a strip cartoon,' said Isobel.

He laughed. 'That's exactly what it is. No detail spared. How are you getting on with the quiz?'

'I'm not,' said Isobel. 'Just picking out bits that might be interesting.'

'Anything I can help you with?'

'Well,' said Isobel, hastily looking down the sheet, 'here's one: "Which animal is directly underneath Lewis Carroll?"'

'Ah, that'll be the Alice window; it's in the Dining Hall on the left as you go in, down towards high table. It's worth seeing.'

Isobel thanked him, then on impulse she said, 'there is one more but I don't suppose you'll know it.'

He looked intrigued. 'Try me.'

'"Who is the friend quoted in the last Harry Potter book?"'

He frowned. 'I haven't read the last one. I expect I will at some point.' He thought for a moment. 'It couldn't be something to do with the film could it? They filmed the Hogwarts Great Hall scenes here in the Dining Hall.'

'I didn't know that,' said Isobel. 'But it says the last book and they haven't filmed that yet.'

'Then I'm sorry; you're right. I've no idea,' he said smiling at her. 'I must go now; I'm expected home. Enjoy the rest of your visit to Christ Church.'

Isobel watched him go with a sudden rush of disappointment that surprised her. Had she been attracted to him? She had certainly enjoyed his company. Or was it that he had reminded her more than a little of Guy? She sighed; she'd go to the Dining Hall and find the Alice window.

She made her way back to the south side of the cathedral, down the steps and into the cloisters. How ancient and tranquil it felt here; how wonderful it must have been, she thought, to walk here in peace in the old days, secure in the daily routine of religious life and in what was to come. Or had they, too, reached a point in their lives when they wondered what it all meant, what it was all for?

She was so lost in thought that she hadn't noticed until that moment that she'd arrived at an entrance with steps leading upwards. With an effort she brought herself back to the present and climbed the impressive stone sweep of staircase until she reached the Dining Hall. It was immense, with the high table at the far end and rows of tables at right angles laid for that evening's dinner. She looked around, but couldn't see any of her group. Perhaps they'd done the Dining Hall and were now busy in the shop.

She made her way down the hall. Yes, there was the Alice window, with a portrait of Alice on the left and Lewis Carroll on the right. Immediately below him was the Dodo, and surely down at the bottom was the White Rabbit and that must be the March Hare with the Mock Turtle next to him, and - was that the Duchess?

She was suddenly glad that this weekend, however else it might fail her, had brought her to Christ Church. What a glorious hall. She could understand why they'd chosen it for the film. She walked slowly back, looking at the portraits that lined the walls, and stopped next to a group of people standing by the entrance, listening to a gentleman in a bowler hat who was pointing to one of the portraits.

'On the right here we have John Wesley, founder of Methodism. Above him is William Penn, founder of Pennsylvania, who became a Quaker while he was at Christ Church. And of course, on the left of the door we have a portrait of a very important person. People know him as Lewis Carroll, but not many know that his real name was Charles Lutwidge Dodgson.'

Isobel left them to it and went out of the Dining Hall. As she went down the stone staircase a memory stirred, a fleeting recognition of something that had been said. She frowned in frustration. It wouldn't come. She looked at her watch. The group were meeting at four o'clock for a cup of tea in the café opposite the visitors' entrance. She had a little time yet. She'd walk down Christ Church meadows towards the river, clear her head.

Outside it was windy but sunny and she walked briskly. She'd got rather cold. A marquee off to the right of the path caught her eye, and intrigued by the group of onlookers clustered round the entrance, clearly riveted by what was going on, she made her way towards it.

Peering in, she saw people standing at work benches; some appeared to be drawing round templates, while others wore safety glasses and had what looked like cutters in their hands. One man was lifting up, carefully and by its top edge, a sheet of red glass.

Stained glass making, she realised; so it's still going on. She watched them fitting small pieces of coloured glass on to the templates and itched to join them. That's my next course, she decided on the spur of the moment, the ancient art of stained glass making - and there's a bonus: unlike my embroidery group or this weekend, the majority in there are men!

She smiled at herself. Despite everything, she'd come a long way in the last four and a half years, and yet...

She shivered. It was time to go. She could do with a cup of tea even if she didn't want to be part of the jovial proceedings. She didn't want to be on her own any more either. Company, whatever it was like, would be good for her. She walked back up Christ Church meadows, then, as she turned left towards the exit, it came to her, the memory that had been at the back of her mind.

Of course, that was it. The friend quoted. It wasn't a friend of Harry Potter or anything to do with the film. Another name for Quakers was the Society of Friends. William Penn's portrait was on the wall in the Dining Hall; he was a Quaker, a Friend.

And then she remembered the quotations at the beginning of the book, one of them by William Penn: *'Death is but crossing the world as friends do the seas; they live in one another still.'*

The opening sentence. Her eyes filled with tears again and blurred the images around her. Yet she felt strangely exhilarated, joyful even, as she strode along the path away from the ancient buildings, past the garden of remembrance, and out through the gate.

THE HONOURED GUEST

CHARLES JONES

The old boatman filled the silence.

'Three there, four back,' he exhaled in imagined exhaustion as he settled himself among the fine company. He closed his hands round an imaginary oar to hide the fresh calluses that were a hallmark of his recent adventure.

Moments before, the Queen's bailiff, attended by the pantler whose job it was to see that the guests were fed according to their precedence, had placed the boatman at this table. To make a space, the bailiff had employed his black rod. The staff was the bailiff's constant companion, little thicker than a man's thumb but it stood as high as the man's shoulder and the bailiff was a sturdy, meat-fed man.

The rod was so smooth and straight that some said it must be made from a material drawn from fire. It was certainly too smooth, too straight for any piece of wood but too light to be iron. The rod's victims felt it was the work of the devil, given as a gift to one of his own. It was the terror of all those who served the new queen. Blows would be struck by the unseen bailiff who, clad in black, moved around the household by day and night, announcing his presence with a crash of his cane on a post or wall, unless there was a minor transgressor to punish. Its very presence now guaranteed obedience.

The bailiff had arrived at Islip the previous growing season with the young queen Emma from Normandy and always led the way when she left her chamber. When the queen had been confined - and the women had all agreed that she must be long overdue - the bailiff found more time to administer stripes to those who looked to the winter months for a quieter time.

Now, settled in his place at the centre of the table, the boatman looked towards the empty table where the king would sit. His dining companions looked to the humble arrival who had been promoted above them. These were all men now, as the boatman had displaced one of the two women at the table, and the other had risen and followed her, much to the satisfaction of the bailiff. To fill the lingering silence the boatman rose just a little from the bench, moved his arms in a rowing motion, 'three days to get there.' He sank back to the bench, 'and just four to get back,' hoping they would recognize this achievement. His audience was impassive. 'To come and go to London,' he added.

At that moment a boy set trenchers of bread before them. These were baked hard and the boatman could see they were made from fine flour and roughly shaped to support each man's portion of the meats that were to follow.

This was the cue to place their knives, and for those who possessed them, their metal spoons ready for use. Once again at the centre of attention, the boatman sought to find his knife discretely. He slowly withdrew his humble blade with its handle of twine and slid it onto the scrubbed surface under his hand while others rearranged their slim bladed knives with their carved bone handles, some bound in silver wire, in full view.

Since his return to the king's hall at Islip, he had found the place filled with unaccustomed smells mixed with the wood-smoke that told him of preparations for feasting. Perhaps there was now a royal baby to welcome as Epiphany approached. Other boatmen told how they had been summoned to fetch guests who brought baskets with cheeses, meat pies and gifts.

His transformation from menial boatman to a guest at the royal feast had taken less time than he took to drink a small draught of ale. The boy sent to summon the boatman from his inaccessible lodge over the store, had a robe draped around his neck as he emerged from the ladder into the loft lit by a single flame set inside a sturdy pot and fixed to a beam so that it could not fall. Surprised by this unlikely appearance, the boatman called out. The boy quickly gathered the robe together, and approached the boatman, the robe now on outstretched arms. The boatman hesitated but realized he was to wear it and slipped it over his tunic and hose without understanding or thought. He hesitated before lifting the stout leather belt that still hung like a halter round the boy's neck. The belt lacked any holes so was unfitted to any other's girth.

The boy beckoned him to follow. Lacking the time or the courage to punch a hole to fasten the belt, he made a half-hitch with the engraved strap-end still visible despite folding some of the robe's surplus length over the belt. He was dressed.

As he reached the bottom of the ladder the bailiff stepped towards him. He braced for the blow. How could he explain his attire? Instead he found himself following the bailiff, summoned by a slight nod of the head, into the hall.

The bailiff did not have to tell those at the table who had precedence. No words were exchanged but the pantler knew that all the food for the table should be placed in front of the new arrival. The bailiff took the cuff of the robe that now covered the boatman and held it out over the table where all could observe. He rubbed it gently just as a trader might do to indicate the fine quality of the material, the faultless spinning and perfect weaving for the table-company to admire. Dyed in the wool to make the fabric almost solid black, the master-weaver had created a pattern like the sharp ripples that stand on the surface when a steady wind blows along the wide river. All recognized this garment as defining the status of their dining companion.

Accustomed to converse with those he ferried along the waterways, the boatman was disquieted by the silence in the eyes of his dining companions. He felt obliged to offer an explanation and once started, it was hard to know where to stop, for a story has a beginning and must flow naturally through to its end.

'Three days to row there and four days to row back, that's all he gave me. Three days to go to the king. They didn't tell me how to find him. I should just take my boat to the abbey at Thorney.

'I admit I was terrified whenever the bailiff spoke, for his words were few and given in a tongue that made little sense. Still his words "find the king" were clear enough. Then this noble lord stepped right in front of me, so near that we could touch, but I did not flinch because I saw he had already released the staff which now rested in the crook of his arm. With his own hands he took a small leather bag and secured it around my neck.

'He indicated with three fingers how long the going should take. With his right hand he beckoned, holding up four fingers. Just four days to return and fight the river's flow. "Give to the king" was his final instruction as he tugged the bag that was to be my burden.

'My skiff was drawn well out of the water because of all the heavy rain. I've seen boats washed away and smashed on the weirs made by fishermen so I called out for help, expecting no response. But, thank heaven, my cry was quickly answered for all knew the whereabouts and business of the bailiff and dared not delay.

'The light was already fading on that winter's day. The recent storms had filled the river to make my going easier as my shallow skiff could pass over the weirs, which I knew well from a lifetime of passage along this water. But to go at night? It would be black-dark before I reached the flat meadows of Oxford or the fording place around Osney where the many channels could trap the traveller.

'I fixed the cover of waxed linen that I had stitched from small finds to keep the spray from filling the boat. I was proud of this cover which earned me many fine passengers who knew I could deliver them dry to their destinations.

'Just as I prepared to set off into that winter twilight, there was a shout, which I knew must be for me, since no one else was active. This was a night for wise men to find ale-companions or rest in warm straw. So in the cold clear winter air with the moon promising a good light, I waited, aware of the bone-cold that was to come. I lifted the leather bag that the bailiff had tied around my neck and placed it beneath my shirt. I felt the hard wax that sealed the bag. It was not for me to guess what was inside but I knew from the weight that it was not coins for payment or to buy my way out of trouble.

'Just three days to get there and here I was still and shivering. Then two women ran up with willow-woven baskets covered in cloths and well tied down. They handed each in turn, and saying nothing, ran back towards the comfort of the hall's parlour.

'I could smell that one basket held fresh bread. But such plenty could not be for me, so I stowed temptation below the cover where the sight and smell would not torment my present or future hunger. While I was doing this work at the bow, which is shaped like the end of a spear, sharp but flat, I allowed the water to lift the lightened stern off the bank and carry me into the fast flow in the narrow channel at Islip.'

The boatman fell silent as the gaze of his audience was attracted by new torchlights. Their flickering illuminated gold ornaments that announced the arrival of King Ethelred. He was preceded by his steward who supported a heavy, spike-studded mace on his shoulder. When the king was seated, Queen Emma entered, attended by her bailiff. The queen's party paused at the door. The bailiff tapped his rod on the stone floor and reduced the room to a deferential silence. He scanned the assembly, and even the warriors, hidden in the half-light, seemed cowed by his survey. The king's steward rested the head of his mace on the floor and the bailiff took his place behind his queen.

The sounds of the hall remained mute after the king and queen settled, now surrounded by their top-fire guests. The voice of their royal patron announced the Epiphany feast as boys entered carrying jugs then went around the room for a first-filling of the cups.

The boatman wondered if he should grope below his fine robe to find his wooden bowl which was all he possessed to serve as a drinking vessel, for now all around set out their cups of horn or finely turned wood which each drew from a pouch on his belt. He would have to loosen his new belt to reach the pocket that held his few goods.

The boys began to fill the cups, spilling ale as they moved the heavy jugs between cups with their lightening load. During those moments of indecision and the boys with their ale jars drawing nearer, the hand of the pantler set a cup made of dull metal before the boatman and summoned the boys to fill it. It was a reflex that made the boatman peer towards the bailiff for approval. Lifting the cup he took the ale while the steady gaze from the bailiff, and a small nod, indicated approval.

'Well I was terrified,' the boatman continued, drawing the diners back to his story.

'I did not need to row, for the flow of the river was my master going downstream. My task was only to stay with the fast water. I would not meet any fools coming the other way in the dark; only trappers and fishermen were about at this time of night. It would be safe-going because the Norsemen had left our land with a chest filled with the king's coins and now we could travel in safety. They say our new queen has come as a peace-weaver as she is from Norse settlers.'

The tale of the perils and dangers of the boatman's journey was punctuated by the arrival of meats and pies. These were all set before the boatman and hungry eyes would turn from him to the boiled meats, roast fowl, pies of many layers and thick crusts that were fit to eat. With a growing confidence he would pause when his tale permitted to cut his own portion which he placed on his trencher. Then each guest would take his cut. Any juices would be shared; those with spoons, dipping, while others tore away a part of their trencher to scoop any liquor until the plate was clean. So the story of the boatman went along its course.

A subtlety, in the shape of a stone church, was carried in. It rested on a board that was supported by two posts on the shoulders of four boys. They shuffled to make sure that the sides of pastry, glazed to match the colour of the local stone, were not disturbed. The model of the church was formed like a cross with a short, square tower at the crossing point and with many boiled leaves covering the roof.

All gazed as this gift was carried through the hall and offered to the king. They had heard tales of the stone abbeys that the monks were building over the sea to the south. Now their king had made an oath to build such a church to honour his new queen, who had just given birth to a son. The infant was carried, cradled on a shield, first behind and then in front of the high table for all to pay their respect. When the shouts of 'Edward' ceased, the hall settled to a respectful murmur.

The food was cleared, save for some bones, so they attended the boatman again.

'That is why they are taking all that stone down the river. Did I tell you about the barques that go both day and night down the river?'

The boatman had seen the church they were making. The west minster stood on the monk's island at Thorney where the river Thames carried clear water and good fishing to the abbey-land. Fierce sea-tides brought brackish water into the river further east where the church for Saint Paul stood on the hill at the heart of the ancient, walled city that again served as a place of refuge against the Norse invaders.

'As I said, there are boats filled with stone that discharge on the strand beside old Lundenwic, deserted since the raids. I did not see them at first but noticed that the mud was stirred so I knew there was traffic ahead. But with the dawn-light in my eyes, they called out to me. Old friends. As I caught up and told of my night-journey they lashed my boat to their side so I could take a little sleep beneath the waxed cloth, and wrapped within the strong cloth that I can use for a sail when the wind is with me.

'So there I was asleep and travelling still. There could be no stopping with just three days allowed to get there. After noon a hand pushed a piece of bread, not crumbly barley bread, but wheat bread that one can slice and chew, taken from the basket which the expert knots-men had replaced. We were already close by the busy landings at Henley.

'Refreshed, I left my friends to their steady progress with their load of stone and bent over my oar again moving swiftly so that I could come to Thorney. With the tide at the mouth of this great river ebbing, I made good speed but knew it would be hard work with my oar when the sea pushed the other way to dam the river's flow, for a turn. So I pressed on into another freezing night with some dry straw from the stone-ferry to pad my legs and body.

'It was past the middle of the night when a crier pierced the dark announcing some hour. I had reached the monks' island. With no help to pull my skiff clear, and the mud wider than I could throw a rope, I steered for a small channel where I knew I could be secure. With the tide set to rise soon, I did not want my work undone by the great force of the water that runs there. The moment I felt the mud under the keel, I ran to the stern to lift the bow. But a watchman had been set to look out for my coming, and some herdsmen came quickly through the mud and pushed me to firm ground.

'I lifted the two baskets for them to carry, slipping off my shoes which would have been swallowed by the mud and followed the fellows to their byre. They warmed some water for me to drink and it seemed the next moment it was light when they woke me and told me I must leave the humble warmth of their animals and comfortable straw.

'Just two days, two days, is all the time it had taken to get there. But I could spend all the time I had won, and more, for my return upstream.'

The boatman drained his ale-cup. His listeners exchanged glances.

'So I handed my pouch to the abbot as commanded. He squinted at the seal around the draw strings then left me in his cold stone hall, and in its gloom I was soon asleep again, propping myself against one of the walls, thankful that I still had my river clothing and all the padding in place. Who knows how long it was before they returned but I was now rested. The abbot told me that I must return at once and his attendant handed me a cloth for my journey. I took this and could smell there were some smoked fish that traders brought up the river. This would be a rare treat although I could feel the bread was old, lumpen and a crumbly barley bake.

'Now abbots are versed in scripture but know little of the working of the river. I thought to explain that our departure would be set not by man but the action of the turning tide, but I have carried enough noble men to know that they do not debate such things. So I was led back to my boat. I did not know if I would be swept out towards the landing at Auldwic on the strand and even beyond to the bridge which the Norsemen had many times tried to pull down.

'To my joy I saw the river was low and the sea would soon help to push my skiff back towards Islip. There was even a favourable breeze to fill the sail that I could set on a little mast I rig towards the prow. It would be another dark going but there was enough light shed between the scudding clouds to find a safe passage on this broad river.

'But, seated too near the bow, was a great volume of cloth which I am sure was a woman. She said nothing when I addressed her nor indeed for our long journey together. She was from another land.

'With much shouting from me, the abbot's men and the herdsmen, I managed to get the waxed cloth that would keep all her wrapping from a soaking by the river's spray, plus my sail, from beneath her. She protested but things were settled to my satisfaction with the abbot's man taking a few slight blows from my passenger during this reorganisation. So we were set, although she was still too far forward for her own comfort but some folk won't be told, especially when they don't speak a godly tongue.

'The wind took the sail, the herdsmen lent their power to push and I grasped my oar, preparing to be set free from the mud. Now I should see whether I could get such a load, I mean no disrespect of course, back along this river.

'Things were going well with tide and wind and some moon-shine working with us, for by daybreak we were beyond any influence of the oceans where the waters come and go. But then she stands up. She stands in my little boat, and points to the bank. I shout to tell her to sit down but she now rocks the boat so the water comes close to the boards. I did not understand this madness but to save us I had to obey and crossed to some still water. When she saw that we were going to the bank she crouched down so we would not be tipped out.

'With some difficulty, she, for I was now sure it was a she, grabbed a branch and crawled onto the bank. As she rose to walk I saw that I had in truth, two passengers, with the one very soon to enter the world to judge by her size. So I understood that no rides in a cart or seat on a horse were possible for my lady in her condition. What burden was this journey for both of us!

'I kept the boat on its station but looked for a better stage where this mighty lady, whoever she was, might enter again without tipping us all into the water. So this rowing and landing continued through the days with a favourable wind as my only recompense for all this extra work on the broad reach of the river. My bread was soon gone as I waited at the bank and then toiled to bring my lady, with so many stops for her comfort, all the way to Islip. When the food was gone, I slept at each landing.

'This was no time to tire. My father told me, as every father tells his son, that the axe seeks those too tired to lift his shield. At Maldon I held my own shield and when that was shattered, picked up another as the battle went for the Norsemen and many died around me, too tired to defend themselves. I held my shield until our thane led us away. The river can claim a boat just as quickly as the axe or spear. But my battle with the river looked set to last for five days.'

Mention of Maldon had renewed the focus of his audience as none of his listeners were warriors. None had faced the Norsemen, set behind a shieldwall. Nevertheless, hungry eyes inspected the plate of sweetmeats that was placed before the boatman. Coloured yellow, green, red and white, these crumbly confections had come from inside the subtlety presented to the queen. The bright meat rested on a piece of the paste which had formed one wall for the model of the abbey church. A squared pattern of large stones had been engraved into the paste before it was baked a stone-golden brown. But the boatman's journey had to hasten to its end before this strange food could be tasted. They attended him with a renewed respect, for this was an old warrior.

'The nights passed but we traded a steady, cold wind from the east which filled the sail for a concealment of clouds. One morning brought flurries of snow as we put into the bank. I worked my oar into the mud to hold us on the edge and was asleep when the rocking of my skiff told me that it was time to strain my cold arms. The pain was soon gone as I dipped and pushed. So on we went through each short day, now fighting the flow and seeking the slackest water inside the bends that would lead us up towards Oxford and still waters.

'Whenever my lady arrayed herself I could see that she was in truth fair. Her look was calm and I wondered if this woman was gifted with the same courage given to a man who is set in the shieldwall. She too must face pain and danger from which flight is not an option.'

The boatman paused and carefully selected a small ball coloured red, for he had never seen food of this colour before and took a small bite, not ready for the sweet, floral taste. He reached out for a yellow coloured morsel while his companions digested his tale.

'The narrow channel up to the hall brought fire to my hands as I worked my oar back and forth. I thought I would soon see my bare bones but I had to press on for the time allowed for my transit was passed. My lady now seemed to understand that there could be no more landings along this stretch. Battling through the night, bumping into the bank so that we were nearly dumped into the icicled stream several times, we came slowly towards the hall at dawn.

'Watchers must have been set for as we came towards the flat, slack water by the hall, the bailiff stood at the bank.

What price must I pay for travelling over one extra night? In the dim light of that overcast dawn I had no time to compose fearful thoughts for we must still leave the stream and land with the rush of water ever willing to tip us out.

The dark form of the bailiff advanced, striding through the splashing water. I was too cold, too tired to prepare any defence. But he did not come for me. He had pulled up his robe, folding it in his belt revealing tall boots of a tough tan. He waded towards the skiff even going beyond the height of his boot. He reached for the rope to pull us to the bank. When my lady felt that pull, she turned and then released her cold arms from beneath her cloaks, her gaze fixed on the bailiff. As the keel hit firm ground, the bailiff reached in at the bow and lifted his very own lady out of my skiff and they were gone, their eyes together and her arms around his neck.

'So here I sit among you today.' He gestured toward the plate with his open, calloused hand. His guests now took their share of the sweetmeats.

'So let us welcome the holy babe,' said one diner to which there was a cheer.

'And the new aethling, Edward,' cried another to which there was cheering all around.

'And for all others born at this tide,' added the boatman. But few heard while the cheering continued. The boatman looked towards the bailiff, who smiled.

The feast was done. The boatman lifted the engraved paste that had supported the sweetmeats so that he could tell the men on the stone ferries what he had seen. The great gathering of Epiphany came to its end. The story ended with a chalice, a belted robe and a smile.

Queen Emma from Normandy gave birth to her first child at Islip c 1004. This baby would be known to history as King Edward the Confessor. After the death of his father, King Ethelred, and following his mother's marriage to the invader King Cnut, Edward spent many years in exile. Westminster Abbey, built of Oxford's golden 'free stone', was consecrated days before Edward died in 1066 and where his tomb was identified a thousand years later.

AN OXFORD INTERLUDE

LINORA LAWRENCE

St Hugh's College,
Oxford
16th October 1926

Dear Mum and Dad,

I have arrived safely, as has my trunk! Thank you so much, both of you, for taking me to the station to see me off. I did miss you so when we were waving goodbye.

I am in a room on the third floor. It's quite nice with a view of the garden, though it's not like your garden, Mum – it's very bare. In the middle of the lawn is a little magnolia tree which, apparently, the students planted in 1918 to commemorate the end of the Great War. There is a girl called Eleanor in the room opposite mine; she seems to be my type. She is reading History so she must be brainy! We went into dinner together yesterday evening. It was good to have someone to go with, especially on the first evening. Lunch today felt like school, but dinner is much more formal. There is a funny red-haired girl on the second floor...

St Hugh's College,
Oxford
16th October 1926

Dearest Mother,

Thank you very much for coming all the way into Newcastle to see me off on the train. The journey was pretty fair and I arrived in Oxford more or less on time. My trunk arrived by six o'clock so I can't complain.

I am in a room on the third floor. It's not as big as my bedroom at home but it will be fine when I get my bits and pieces unpacked. There is a girl in the room opposite called Dorothy; she is reading English, lucky thing! We went down to dinner together which as you know, I had been dreading, so I am very glad to have found someone nice so early on. You were very wise to tell me to pack two bars of soap; I have had to lend one to someone already! She is a girl on the second floor with bright russet hair. She won't tell us her first name and says everyone calls her by her surname – Pickles...!

> St Hugh's College,
> Oxford
> 16th October 1926

Dear Ma and Pa,

Just a line to let you know I am settled in. Thank you for motoring me over to Oxford. It was a big help, though annoyingly my trunk hasn't yet arrived so I am a little stuck for some things. I would have thought the college would have provided soap! I had to borrow some from a girl upstairs. I have enquired, and there is a piano on which I can practise and a better one in the house next door (called the Lawn) which is part of the college; some second years live in it. Miss Gwyer thinks I can use that too. I am sorry I shall be away for your birthday, Ma, but I shall write again nearer the time.

> With love,
>
> Evelyn

Beyond having a vague feeling that it should be a bit like the Sixth Form, none of the girls had a very clear idea of what to expect from their first term at college. Tutorials were quite different from school: hour long sessions with a tutor, usually one to one. Dorothy had a female tutor who filled her with so much terror that she vomited up her breakfast before going to a nine o'clock tutorial.

Eleanor had nice Mr Stamper who lived in a college house in Long Wall Street, one of the oldest houses in Oxford.

'You should be doing English,' sighed Dorothy after Eleanor had practised an essay on her. 'You have a way with words.'

'I wanted to, you know; that was my first love,' replied Eleanor.

'So, what happened?' asked Dorothy.

'My Headmistress more or less insisted I didn't,' said Eleanor. 'She said most girls choose English and it would lessen my chances of getting in. History was my next best subject so that was it.'

'Was St Hugh's your first choice?'

'No, except that I didn't really make a choice. Miss Gurney made the decisions. Her first choice for me was Girton, Cambridge, but that was only because she had been there. Anyway I didn't get in, and then Miss Walpole, my history teacher, thought of here.'

'My first choice was Lady Margaret Hall,' confided Dorothy. 'They didn't take me, but they did suggest I might fit in here.'

'Well, I'm jolly glad you *are* here,' said Eleanor, 'but I wonder why they didn't want you at LMH?'

'Hmm, I got the impression you've got to be practically related to a bishop, or at least a clergyman to get in. They are very Church of England and I don't think they thought much of my family.'

'Are you not C of E?'

'I'm not anything really. My father wouldn't have me or my brother christened and he had us taken out of RI classes at school. He thought we should come to it fresh as adults and make up our own minds. I used to sit out of classes with the Jewish girls and do revision.'

'Gosh, didn't that make it hard for exams? Weren't there things you didn't know?'

'There certainly were,' replied Dorothy. 'I had to have a lot of extra coaching when we knew I had a chance of university.'

'I went to school with a girl called Nonny,' volunteered Eleanor. She was registered by her father as 'Anonymous'. He believed she shouldn't be saddled with a name she didn't like and that she should choose one herself when she was grown-up! Of course she had to be called something and she just became Nonny.'

Thoughts of school faded as the eight weeks of term sped by. The end of the second week of December was suddenly upon them and the girls went home for Christmas.

Hilary term was, by far, the toughest term. Winter weather saw the usual outbreak of colds and infections. The girls discovered the good offices of Miss Salt, the matron - some were destined to see more of her than others. Maids struggled up and down the stairs with coal buckets for the fires which the girls sat huddled round, clutching toasting forks and trying to study.

The beginning of March saw much better weather and the students seemed to come back to life. An unexpected invitation was pushed under Eleanor's and Dorothy's doors.

10th March 1927

Dear E and D

I would love to invite you both to tea. I have discovered a nice tea shop at 129 High Street. It is called the Noted Café and is not very far down on the right. I thought Friday afternoon, as we are all free from tuts then, about half past three. Do say you will come.

Pickles

Slightly wondering why they had been asked but, nevertheless, pleased, the girls duly met up and Pickles spent an hour and a half charming them, entertaining them and generally being lots of fun. They walked back to college together in high spirits – Pickles had 'taken them up'!

St Hugh's College,
Oxford
16th March 1927

Dearest Mother,

...We had a lovely tea at the Noted Café. Toasted crumpets and even you would have said it was a good cup of tea! However, Dorothy and I have now worked out why we were invited. Do you remember the paragraph in the Rules which laid out the chaperone system – I said it would never apply to me as I would never go anywhere and would just study? Well, it seems Pickles has been asked out and she needs at least one of us to be a chaperone. Pickles says she is not going to give up having a social life for three years, so she needs girl friends to make up a foursome, or even a group of six. Dorothy has been brave and said 'yes' to the first event. I wonder if I shall ever dare...

Easter came and went followed by the joys of Trinity term - the warm weather, the light evenings and the knowledge that the whole summer lay ahead. In the first week of term Pickles said she would come with Eleanor to Blackwells. Eleanor was searching for a history book that could help her with an essay on the Hundred Years War and Pickles was searching for - what? For someone who was studying Mathematics she was showing a surprising willingness to hang around the second floor, flicking through some books but keeping a weather eye on who was coming up the stairs. Some students wearing their college scarves came past; one in particular stood out, blond, a little taller than the others. He walked purposefully to the back of the section. Pickles positioned herself and continued to browse through the life of Cardinal Richelieu. The blond god evidently found the book he required, said something to his companion, and turned in the direction of the till. Pickles hastily replaced the Cardinal and moved over to

Eleanor saying very clearly, 'Have you found the book you want?'

Eleanor looked up just in time to see the young god stoop to pick up a lace edged handkerchief with the initials EAP in one corner. 'Excuse me, I think you may have dropped this.'

'Oh dear, how silly of me,' Pickles dropped her eyelids and then raised them again, her eyes meeting his. 'How kind of you.' She opened her bag, 'Is that a Lincoln scarf?'

'How clever of you to know.'

'They are very distinctive.'

'Are you at college too? May I ask where?'

'Not many to choose from in our case,' smiled Pickles. 'I might make you guess – but that would be unkind wouldn't it?' She replaced the proffered handkerchief in her bag and simultaneously withdrew a small object which she put in the boy's hand. 'My card,' she said.

'She's had cards made up!' gasped Eleanor recounting the whole scene to Dorothy. 'I couldn't believe my eyes!'

'I thought only our mothers had cards,' sighed Dorothy.

The blond god turned out to be called Bernard, a sociable chap, who soon became central to group events. The ever-improving weather meant picnics and punting on the river, concerts at various colleges - sometimes the Sheldonian - and walking home in the long, light evenings in time to beat the curfew.

St Hugh's College,
Oxford
3rd May 1927

Dearest Mother,

...You will never guess what happened last night. You remember we are expected to dine in our own college every evening? Well, that means if we do meet up with someone it generally is for afternoon tea. More and more often recently, Pickles has been late for dinner; tea-time seems to go on for hours for her. You know how if we are late entering the dining hall we have to wait and catch the Principal's eye (or whoever is standing in for her) then we bow to apologise, she nods and that means we are allowed to sit down. Well, last night Pickles was late, yet again. She came in and waited, and tried to catch Miss Gwyer's eye and she just wouldn't look at her. She kept her standing for the whole meal! Well, she did slide out just before the end and none of us saw her again for the rest of the evening. Oh gosh, I would have died if that had happened to me...!

The summer of 1927 saw the girls going their separate ways, home for the Long Vacation, never to be freshers again.

> Higham Dykes,
> Milborne,
> Northumberland
> 29th June 1927

Dear Dorothy,

Thank you for your last letter. I agree the first few days at home felt strange. Now it all seems back to normal. I think the family imagine I have all the time in the world to help Mother and go visiting with her, but she does understand. I am making a routine of going into the Lit and Phil (Literary and Philosophical Society Library) in town every week. They do lend out, though some of the books I need are reference only. They really are my only source up here, apart from ordering from Blackwell's. How are you finding it in Derbyshire...?

> 19 Bakewell Road,
> Buxton,
> Derbyshire
> 28th September 1927

Dear Eleanor,

It won't be very long before we see each other again. It's going to be rather different isn't it? You'll be in The

Lawn and I'll be in College. Still, it is only a walk across the garden so we mustn't let it make any difference. According to the list, Pickles is being put in The Lawn too, so she will be nearer her beloved piano. You know she never replied to my letter. Did she ever reply to you? Weybridge isn't the ends of the earth after all...

October the 12th saw the girls back, on familiar territory now, surrounded by friends, and their study patterns and social lives established. Finals seemed ages away and the world was their oyster.

Pickles was charming her way through boy after boy. Bernard had been a faithful beau from the beginning, but now in his third year he was beginning to worry about finals. He wrote to her, ending their friendship. Pickles was miffed to say the least; normally she did the ending! She tossed the letter into Eleanor's lap. 'Read it for yourself,' she said petulantly.

'But he's only worrying about his finals,' said Eleanor, reading the letter carefully. 'He says his father has been coming down hard on him.'

'If he really cared for me he wouldn't let that matter!'

'But, do you really care for him?' Eleanor dared to ask.

'I don't know; I might do. I don't want to have to make up my mind at this stage.'

'Well, why don't you write back and tell him that?' suggested Eleanor. Pickles didn't reply but looked thoughtful.

Two days later she was back. 'Couldn't you please draft the letter for me? You are so good with words, everyone says so. I trust you completely. I could just do the final copy and sign it and send it.'

It had to be admitted that Eleanor was flattered to be turned to and unfortunately there was no one older and wiser on hand to suggest that this might be dangerous territory. The letter was painstakingly drafted, full of understanding, suggesting they didn't burn their boats, but put all socialising on hold. At least until Bernard had sat his finals and indeed knew his results. Even after that, he could concentrate on whatever he was going to do next while she, Evelyn, concentrated on her final year.

Bernard read the letter with great joy. Evelyn had depths after all. She really did understand the serious side of life as well as being damnably attractive. He believed she had hinted as much as a well-brought-up young lady could hint that she was prepared to wait nearly two years for him. Fired up, he decided to act. He arranged to meet Pickles in the Botanic Gardens, turned up with a bouquet of flowers and proposed. It would have to be secret, of course. Pickles had never dreamed of waiting for anyone, but being proposed to was flattering, very flattering, so in the romance of the moment, she accepted.

Naturally, word got around amongst their group of friends. A couple of weeks later Eleanor bumped into Bernard coming out of the Bodleian Library. Both of them felt slightly embarrassed.

'I haven't seen much of you lately,' said Eleanor, instantly regretting her words.

Bernard shifted from one foot to the other and back again. 'We've all been a bit tied up,' he volunteered, 'George, Andrew and I. Truth is Vincent's got himself into a bit of a state.' Vincent was an intense young man in their 'set' but quiet and always slightly on the edge of it, 'Fact is he's very low, very low indeed. We've formed a rota; we never leave him alone. Andrew's with him now in the Library and he'll make sure he has some lunch. We're taking it in turns sitting up with him all night... just to make sure... just in case.'

Eleanor stared in horror. 'How awful,' she said. What brought this on?'

Again Bernard looked embarrassed. 'Well, the news - the secret news; when he heard, well, he's hardly spoken since.'

Eleanor nodded, 'I'm sorry, so dreadfully sorry,' she stammered.

'Hardly your fault, old girl,' said Bernard manfully. 'It was all in his own head you know, Evelyn never encouraged him.'

'Oh, didn't she', Eleanor thought to herself – not aloud to Bernard of course. She smiled weakly, but couldn't think of an answer.

'Well, better get on,' he gave her a half-hearted wave and set off.

Eleanor walked back to college lost in thought. She told herself that at least Bernard and Pickles were happily engaged - but were they? It was during that walk along Broad Street, right into St Giles and on up the Banbury Road that Eleanor had an inkling that maybe the wonderful understanding letter she had drafted had not been such a good idea after all. This proved to be right - even before a ring was chosen, the 'engagement' was simply to peter out.

The Christmas vacation came and went. The girls returned with the usual coughs and colds, and Miss Salt had her hands full with syrups and steam kettles.

St Hugh's College,
Oxford
20th February 1928

Dearest Mother,

I promised I would write and tell you when the first crocuses flowered in St Mary Magdalen's churchyard; well, they have this week. I know it will be ages yet before they're out at home. They are up in the garden at college too; you can just see the colour they are going to be, but they are not quite out yet. It's funny how Mary Mag's is always first. There is a nice bit of news to tell you. Dorothy's parents have sent her money for her birthday next week; some of it is to buy leather gloves and some of it is for three of us to go out to tea. We are going to Elliston and Cavells which is similar to Fenwicks at home. Dorothy has asked me specially to go with her to choose the gloves and then we will invite Pickles to join us for tea in their tea rooms. I am so looking forward to it.

Eleanor and Dorothy got off to a bad start. In their ignorance they attempted to enter by the door reserved for the wives of dons, and presumably others of that standing, but were directed to the public entrance by a uniformed doorman. Either girl on her own might have given up, but together they braved their way to haberdashery and leather goods. Such an array: black, navy, brown and tan. Amidst all of these was a pair of beautiful lilac gloves, perhaps left over from the previous summer. Dorothy fell in love with them but knew her mother would never approve. After an inward battle she selected some navy blue with a silk lining and the girls took themselves off to tea to mark the occasion. Pickles joined them for the tea and presented Dorothy with an autograph album. 'Look, I've started it,' she said. 'I am on the first page.' Indeed, there it was, a pretty sketch of kittens and tangled balls of wool. She had given it the title 'Mother's Little Helpers' - what wasn't she good at?

'I would have chosen the lilac gloves,' said Pickles. 'After all it was a birthday present!'

'Yes, but mother would have wanted me to be practical. I just know she wouldn't have approved of the others.'

'You might have marked them the first time you wore them and then you would have been upset,' said Eleanor. She had bought Dorothy violets from Gees the flower shop within a conservatory just down the road from St Hugh's. To match, she had added a box of Yardley's violet soap. It had seemed so clever when she planned it, but now felt a little tame next to the autograph album.

The second and last summer was under way. The Long Vac was dominated by reading lists and the knowledge that finals were now in sight.

Michaelmas Term 1928 found Eleanor and Dorothy living out in a boarding house in Norham Gardens. It was run by a Miss Hurleston and, since the occupants were all St Hugh's girls, was very much an extension of college.

27 Norham Gardens,
Oxford
20th October 1928

Dearest Mother,

Miss Hurleston reminds me of Aunty Edie. She wears skirts down to her ankle boots and wears her hair in 'headphones' round her ears. A funny thing happened to Dorothy. Miss Hurleston, spotting a pot of Pond's Cold Cream on her dressing table, sniffed audibly and remarked that there was nothing wrong with soap and water. We all adore her dog. It is a little Sealyham and he is her one weak spot. If he likes us then Miss Hurleston is quite alright, but anyone who is not a dog person is just tolerated!

Early bad weather set in and many were again struck down with infections which once they had a hold, took many weeks to eradicate. Whooping Cough was going round and a number of students succumbed. The uncontrollable coughing weakened them to the point of requiring true nursing which the college could not undertake to do. The worst sufferers were sent home to recuperate. This included Eleanor.

Higham Dykes,
Milbourne,
Northumberland
1st December 1928

Dear Dorothy,

I am sorry I haven't written before now. I have just felt so weak and exhausted. Mother keeps making egg custards and beef tea. Please forgive me if I keep this short, but do write and tell me any news. It will cheer me up and I won't feel so far away from everything...

27, Norham Gardens,
Oxford
16th December 1928

Dear Eleanor,

...Pickles is actually working and not going out very much. We did have tea out together last week and she was asking after you. On a related subject, Bernard had been seen with a young lady from St Hilda's – they seemed quite close according to Mary who saw them in Broad Street. So much for him saying he is 'working like stink'. Still, it was only Mary's interpretation of what she saw. Guess what I found out the other day. Emily Davison was at St Hugh's! Perhaps you knew that. I didn't. You know who I mean, don't you? The suffragette who flung herself in front of the King's horse at the Derby in 1913? It's funny to think she studied here (same as me, English Lang and Lit). Apparently she would have got a first class honours if women had been given degrees then. I suppose she must have been here about ten years before us...

Higham Dykes,
Milbourne,
Northumberland
4th January 1929

Dear Dorothy,

I am just writing to warn you that the doctor has recommended that I don't try to come back to college until the end of January. Although I am better I am still very weak and washed out so he and Mother think a few more weeks of convalescing. I will read of course, but the weather is too bad to attempt travel. We are snowed in as I write; being ten miles out of Newcastle makes all the difference. No buses are running and Carter Bar is blocked. It happens most years, of course. I expect you have it quite bad in Derbyshire too...?

27, Norham Gardens,
Oxford
21st January 1929

Dear Eleanor,

I do miss you not being here. It feels very strange but I do totally understand and I am longing to see you at the beginning of February. Someone else who hasn't come back is Pickles! I didn't realise at first but after four evenings with her not at dinner... No one seems to know anything...

February saw Eleanor's return and she and Dorothy found an opportunity to speak to the Principal, Miss Gwyer. She looked distressed and paused before answering, 'Miss Pickles won't be returning – at all. In fact, she isn't Miss Pickles any longer; it seems she got married during the last summer vacation.'

The girls were too shocked to speak. They all knew the rules. There was no question of undergraduates being allowed to marry during their three years at the university.

Eventually Eleanor said bravely, 'May we be allowed to know her married name?' Miss Gwyer could see from their shocked faces that they had known nothing about it, and that this was a genuine question.

'She is Mrs Miller now. I expect you can write to her care of her parents.'

Eleanor and Dorothy sat over Miss Salt's coal fire with toasted crumpets and tea and talked and talked. 'She always was a flighty one,' said Miss Salt sagely. 'I'm surprised and yet I'm not surprised, if you know what I mean.'

'But to throw everything away, couldn't she have waited just a bit longer?' mused Dorothy.

'She'll always fall on her feet that one,' replied Miss Salt. 'It was someone she met at home, nothing to do with Oxford, apparently. I suppose he wouldn't wait and she thought he was too good to let him get away.'

Dorothy and Eleanor would not have put it as crudely as that but in their hearts they thought Miss Salt was probably right. It seems another of the girls had spotted a tiny lump under Pickles' blouse; she had been wearing her wedding ring on a chain round her neck, but no one ever learned how the college officially found her out.

In May 1929 Dorothy and Eleanor started to sit their finals. When they had first arrived in Oxford, three years had sounded like a lifetime, yet here it was practically over. They would get on with their lives, whatever their results. Dorothy would teach. Eleanor wasn't sure what she would do, except that it wouldn't be teaching. Her dream was to run an academic bookshop, a small version of Blackwell's, but there wasn't any call for one in Newcastle which, besides an excellent medical school, offered only a technical college. She doubted her father, a shrewd businessman, would back such a venture.

All too soon their time as Oxford undergraduates had come to an end, and goodbyes had been said. As they travelled home, both took with them the memory of Miss Gwyer's speech at the final evening reception.

'You will always be members of St Hugh's College. I don't expect you to appreciate, at the moment, how much this will mean to you. The friendships you have made, the common bonds you share, the life-long links forged during your stay here, will serve as a solid foundation from which you will step out in to the world. You have been taught how to learn, and I hope you will continue to do so for the rest of your lives.'

THE LOST COLLEGE

CHRIS BLOUNT

'Worcester, Balliol, Wadham? Peter, I bet you a pint I'll guess it within five,' said Tristan.

'You'd never have heard of it.'

'Never heard of it? I know all thirty-nine colleges, their foundation dates, their coats of arms, their - I studied them all. I wrote a thesis on college history. I can even tell you about Manchester Hargreaves.'

'Harris Manchester,' George corrected him.

'OK, OK, it's been a long time. Then there's St Hugo's, Temple Bar.'

'Tristan, that's an investment trust!'

'And that coal-mining town.'

Peter was already regretting his decision to have a drink with the other alumni. In fact, no one at Barratt's Bank had known he had a degree from Oxford until he wore the cricket tie. He had never really clicked with the ostentatious Tristan, manager of Barratt's Special Situations Fund. Special Sits just about summed up Tristan Francis Colley. TFC he called himself. T for Too and C for Cool, and, well, you can guess the rest.

Peter was the manager of the calmer, more respectable - some would say boring - Bond Fund. He sometimes had a drink with George and Perry, who were at Oxford at the same time and had also been enticed into this 'academic elite' grouping.

While Tristan went to the bar, George continued the interrogation in a more gentle manner.

'So what was your college?'

'No really, George, it doesn't exist any more.'

'But no colleges have closed since, well, ever. Or maybe there was one in the 1890s - I'm not sure.'

'OK, but keep it from Tristan, especially in view of his inconsistent expertise on college history. There was a college called St Clements, founded and provisionally approved in 1990. It was only going to be properly recognised once it had been in existence for a full three-year undergraduate cycle. The authorities did it that way because of its dubious funding. Have you heard of SOCS? No, it wasn't a rival to the Bullingdon or the Assassins. It stands for the Society of Cognitive Scientists. Almost any weird idea could earn you membership of SOCS. It was founded by a reclusive American called Latoo Pernan, Iranian by birth, who had a fascination with the occult. He'd made a fortune from porn mags and casinos - though Oxford didn't know that at the time.'

'Nice bit of crumpet over there,' said Tristan, returning with the drinks. 'Times four, one each.' This apparently referred to the girls not the lagers. Tristan sat down and took a huge gulp, only half of which went down his throat, the other half splashing into a compromising position on his lap, suggesting the early onset of incontinence. 'Shit. Only just back from the cleaners today.'

'The suit or its owner?' said Perry, thinking that neither looked to have been cleaned or pressed for months.

Tristan, oblivious, pursued his enquiry. 'Did I hear you say SOGS?'

'Yes. South Oxfordshire Golfing Society.'

'You don't look like a golfer to me.'

'I only play a few times a year,' said Peter, fearing yet another of Tristan's hobby horses.

'Can't stand the game, though I suppose I might try it once I've given up pointing guns at things with wings.'

'Soon, I hope,' said George.

Tristan retired to the loo in search of a hand-drier for his trousers. It didn't take an Oxford degree to deduce that, with World Dryer's immovable nozzle pointing to the floor from a height of five foot, and the offending garment located around two foot six, it would require Tristan to undress or, being vertically challenged, use a stool to dry himself off.

In the bar, the others were grateful for his absence.

'I can trust you guys,' said Peter, 'but a Worcester man like Tristan? Tell him and you might as well have a debate at the Union. Anyway, the idea was to fill the college with inventors who would provide a source of income to the college and prestige to Oxford. It was only small - fifty undergraduates, no postgrads - and all supplied by SOCS. The intention was to have no outsiders, but owing to an admissions error three of us had places elsewhere and our colleges were oversubscribed. I was reading metaphysics so that fitted in very well, and the other two did electronics.'

'So where was St Clements, and what happened to the building?' said Perry.

At that moment Tristan returned - apparently dry - with further evidence of inebriation.

'Made me, Oxford did,' he shouted, hoping the clientele of the Old Bull would be suitably impressed. But the drinkers were mainly City traders and would be more inclined to think he was bragging of some insider deal. While he was quick on City gossip, be it social or financial, and would use it to his advantage, Tristan's powers of retention were limited. Hence he was well suited to Special Sits. It was a mystery, however, how he had scraped a degree in Ancient History. A mystery, that is, until George had discovered that Tristan had wooed a young history don.

Tristan turned back to Peter. 'You don't look like an Oxford man to me. Never seen a tie like that before. All the college cricket ties are in the Bear, some torn, some stained, but they're all there. You see I don't believe you. I think you and your college and your cricket tie and your golf society are a sham; I don't think you ever went to Oxford. I think you flashed a bogus degree at Barrett's and finished up - '

George stopped him in full lager flow. 'And of course your degree was achieved honourably?'

'Well no one gets a two-one without a little help, unless they are a complete genius who never fondled a gun or a girl.'

'Not to mention a little grade inflation in the degree department,' added George. 'Tris, I think you've had enough.'

'Course I haven't, you silly little shit. I'm just going to get another little round, just two little drinkies, one for meeeee and the other for, well, meeeee. None of you little schmalz could manage another I'm sure.'

It may have been the sudden movement as he staggered from the table, or perhaps the prospect of another lager and another scotch to which his stomach objected, but the woman at the next table, earlier the subject of his lust, now became the unfortunate target of his vomit. The girl's escort, no stranger to the gym, lifted Tristan and threw him across the bar.

Much later, after a brawl involving several drinkers, the bar manager, two policemen and a placatory donation from Tristan to the woman, the graduates left, Tristan having suffered cuts and bruises but nothing broken except his reputation for holding his drink.

Peter vowed not to repeat the Old Bull experience. He could not avoid Tristan in the daily course of investment management, but he kept conversation to a minimum.

Then, some months later and with Tristan safely on holiday or at the Priory, George suggested the two of them meet for a drink.

'You were right,' said George, 'St Clements College did exist. I found references to it in the *Gazette*.'

Peter was surprised, but supposed that the college's students would have to use the small ads like any other.

'But where was it?' persisted George.

'Maybe it's time I told you the whole story. What are you doing on Saturday? Fancy a trip to Oxford?'

Peter and George alighted from the bus opposite the Angel & Greyhound. Over a pint of bitter and a panini, Peter continued his story.

'You see, SOCS began to get involved in some pretty strange out-of-body experiments. I was not a party to any of this, and nor were most of the undergrads, for whom life went on as normal with a few lectures, a rare tutorial and the usual East Oxford student gigs. A few SOCS students dropped out or, at any rate, were never seen again after a couple of terms. One of the dons had an unexplained terminal illness, and as I said, nobody was working very hard, so nobody was too bothered. It was in our final year, November 1992, that it all came to a head.'

'That's the year I came up - and met Tris,' said George.

'Well, it was about then that stories started to circulate that SOCS was experimenting in eugenics at St Clements. The authorities became very worried and several dons left mid-year - unheard of.'

'Was one of them called Theo?'

'How the hell do you know that?'

'You might not believe this but Tris was OK then - funny, but not such a pompous arse. He seemed to appeal to women. They found him amusing which made up for him being so short. Anyway, there was this stunningly pretty blonde, Matilda, who we were all trying to impress but to no avail. For some reason Tris hadn't been around when Matilda first appeared on the scene but when they met there was no stopping her. Tris didn't even have to try. They were a serious item all that term. She was reading Ancient History like Tris. And of course apart from us she had other admirers, one of whom was a young don called Theo. I don't know if she was two-timing but Tris certainly thought so. Theo was obsessed with Matilda. Towards the end of that term Theo and Matilda just disappeared. They never came back to Oxford. Rumour was that she was pregnant - you can imagine Tris's reaction - and that they got married and went to live in France. But why? It's not that much of a scandal. Theo wasn't at the same college; Matilda wasn't one of his pupils; he was only twenty-eight and she was nineteen. It just didn't add up. Tris disguised his feelings with a drinking binge and was arrested for setting fire to a university building. I think that was St Clements. For some reason the charges against him were dropped. No one was burnt, but it was clearly arson. He has always refused to discuss the whole incident, even with me. He is in denial that Matilda, Theo and St Clements ever existed. That's why he went ballistic when he saw your tie in the Old Bull. And of course, there is now no trace and virtually no record of the college.'

'That would fit,' said Peter. 'There were lots of rumours at the time, most of them more fanciful than that. Theo was definitely a St Clements don, though I have no idea what his subject was. Part of me wants to uncover the whole story, part of me wants to forget it.'

'So where was the college?'

'Well, here. Just outside, underneath the car park and, er, that revolting red Lego building.'

'You mean they built the Flo - '

'Never say that word. All the letters are significant to SOCS.'

'OK, but they built it on top?'

'Look it's not really a proper building at all. It's just a semi-circle of student accommodation.'

They stepped outside into the car park.

'Can you see any evidence of any building ever having been here?'

'No.'

'They covered it up well. Tarmac is a good disguise, especially when it's covered with cars most of the time. There are some odd bumps as they couldn't dig it all out, but it's on a slope and there are plenty of tree roots, so who would notice?'

'It would be a great story.'

'Sure, but there are plenty of people around to suppress it and they're still high up in the university, not to mention the movers and shakers at SOCS.'

'So what was here?'

'St Clements was little more than a collection of early twentieth century villa-type properties, rather like the ones round the corner in Iffley Road. A converted Methodist Hall served as the main building. Some of the houses were under the Flo - building. I prefer to call it the new Queen's College building. The car park was mainly garden and low-level sheds which were used as labs. The authorities were desperate for a solution. They had a bit of luck because Queen's was equally desperate to provide more student accommodation. The university said it had just the site and would pay. How could they say no?'

'How did they get round planning permission?'

'They fast-tracked all that. Remember the whole university's reputation was at stake. Eugenics, possible murders, taking money from a dubious source. Oxford couldn't handle that. They covered the old buildings with huge sheets, demolished them in a few days, worked day and night on the new building; remember it is only half a building. Suddenly the walls were up by the beginning of term and it was opened a year later by the Queen Mother - little did she know!'

'I could just about buy that, but no evidence and no leak?'

'SOCS is still powerful. My guess is that there are senior figures at the university still on Latoo Pernan's payroll. And SOCS pays for things other universities can only dream of. Anyway, there *is* some evidence still. Do you need to get rid of that pint?'

'Sorry?'

'In the gents. On the car park. You see the toilet block?'

'Yes.'

'Quite new individual cubicles, doors straight out on to the ramp from the car park?'

'Yes.'

'Look at the one on the far left. It's different, right?'

'Can't see any difference.'

'Well you will. That's the one we're going to use. Only I *am* going to have to go first.'

Peter went inside, reassured himself the evidence was still there and let George have his turn.

'It's the original cistern,' exclaimed George when he emerged, 'from one of the demolished houses.'

'Not just the cistern, the whole cubicle! The stonework has been rendered and then the brickwork has been built round it.'

'But why did they leave it? Can't just be the pretty plumbing.'

'I really don't know,' said Peter. 'But I wouldn't want to stay long in there. There is a very strange sensation after about 30 seconds, and I think a buzzing, like tinnitus. My feeling is there is a powerful gas between the walls but I can't prove it, and I can hardly test it by driving a JCB into it.'

'I have no sense of direction,' said George. 'How long was I in there, Peter?'

'Forty-two seconds.'

'I can't tell you where the road is or where the traffic is coming from.'

'Easy to have an accident, and there are traffic wardens for the car park day and night, even though there is no charge after six thirty.'

'So?'

'Because we are not the only people who have our suspicions. The toilet block is often locked throughout the day for no apparent reason. Now let me show you something else.'

They walked next door to the red building, but as usual there was no one in the porters' lodge and they went through into the garden. The semicircular building, though roofed and occupied, cried out for someone to complete it. In the middle of the semicircle was a piece of elevated lawn. A few steps led up to a strange object standing in the middle of the grass on a brick base. A circular metal frame covered by a leathery fabric was attached to the main post and waved slightly in the wind. It had no obvious purpose; there was no description of any kind.

'What is it?' said George.

'Ask the next student you see.'

As they went out of the building, George found a fresh-faced student and asked him if he knew what the strange design on the lawn was for.

'I have no idea,' he said, 'but we call it Matilda.'

RABBIT FENLEY AND THE BODY IN THE GARDEN

SHEILA COSTELLO

In life old Harry Sefton had been a difficult man, in death he proved worse. The sale of his home in a pleasant cul-de-sac in Cumnor near Oxford was made unduly complicated by the presence of his remains in the back garden. Mr Sefton, true to form, had insisted on being buried in the spot where he had pruned his roses and passed his days quarrelling with the neighbours and swearing at their children.

When the property came onto the books of Cooper and Tyne, Evan Stubbs, detailed to look after the business, had to down a quarter bottle of whisky before rising to the challenge. He couldn't fault the place itself, it had many attractive features and if a prospective buyer did chance to enquire, he sang the praises of its lattice-style windows and herringbone paths.

'Front and rear,' he told Brad and Kate Drake on their initial viewing, 'front and rear. And at the side there's a small glasshouse that catches the sun. Very good for growing tomatoes. The gentleman who used to own it was a keen gardener. It's a perfect first-time buy.'

The Drakes, not long married, were looking for a bargain, Evan Stubbs for a quick sale. You could put as much of a gloss as you pleased on 22 Baynard Way but it was a distinct liability with its former occupant skulking in the flowerbed. In Evan Stubbs's opinion, had it not been for the vagaries of the market it was unlikely that anyone would have touched the place. But the body in the garden brought the price down considerably.

Tactfully, he drew Brad Drake to one side, fingered his lilac tie and asked, 'Does your good lady - does she suffer with her nerves?'

'I don't know,' said Brad. 'Do you suffer with your nerves, Kate?'

'Not that I've noticed.' The reply came from between a pair of lips as thin as string beans.

'Because,' Evan Stubbs chose his words carefully, 'there is a slight drawback to this property for all its charm. Mr Sefton, the original owner, was devoted to his garden. It was a stipulation of his will that he be buried in the place that he loved most. An old law permits this.'

'And so the person in question is now...?' said Kate Drake.

'Under the geraniums to the right of the fence,' murmured Evan Stubbs.

Of Mrs Sefton, who had had her body compared to a kitchen vegetable patch and her breasts to cabbages by the manic gardener, nothing was said. Mrs Sefton had once attempted to dispose of her husband by spraying ant killer on his cornflakes. The attempt failed. During the subsequent divorce negotiations she sullenly agreed to renounce her interest in the property rather than talk to the police. She had not been seen in the area since but the postman got it into his head to spread a rumour that she was somewhere down in Botley, brooding on her wrongs. After her departure, the old man revised his will, naming a cousin as heir and charging him with the execution of his final request. The cousin was eager to exchange his inheritance for cash. He also had a passion for geraniums.

Evan Stubbs, faced with the task of explaining the mysteries of the geranium bed, felt put upon and oppressed and drew his breath in sighs as if he was ashamed of the whole clammy business.

But the Drakes bought the place. They were young and punchy and couldn't afford to be too particular. Their joint earnings as a college librarian and a printmaker were modest and Evan Stubbs's manner - desperation mingled with cupidity - made them laugh.

They speedily redecorated the house. Out went the old wallpaper with its pattern of huge, unbelievable dahlias; in came Mexican rugs and dishes with a spiral design, a pine table and matching benches and a clock whose mechanical parts were exposed. The Drakes got acquainted with the crowd at the local pub and were regulars at quiz nights where the body in the garden was the subject of endless jokes. They called him the lodger, discussed whether they should charge him rent or whether they should bag him up and trade him off as compost. They were quite up front about it all.

When the Fenleys, who were new to the area, came round for a meal one evening, in between the soup and the saddle of lamb Brad Drake rubbed his hands and, to give the conversation a boost, said jovially, 'Well, the stiff's kept himself to himself as yet, I'll allow him that. He's not acted up in the slightest.'

Scott Fenley, horrified, threw his arm around his wife's shoulder. 'Can we change the topic? Rabbit's highly strung, you know.'

She was a small, rather twitchy woman who sat nestled against her husband and showed no concern at being called Rabbit. But now she said, more staunchly than might have been imagined, 'Oh, I'm not that bad.'

Scott Fenley clamped the little thing to him. 'Come along there, sweetheart. You know the teeniest upset has you hyperventilating.'

The host passed round a tray of drinks and the hostess pushed a dish of creamed potatoes through the serving hatch.

'Potatoes, Rabbit,' said Scott Fenley, rushing to fetch the dish, 'creamed potatoes, your favourite. Do you think you could manage a double helping?'

Rabbit said she'd try. 'And I wonder,' she mused, 'if the body out there is decomposing?'

'Rabbit!' Scott Fenley accidentally doused his broccoli in mint sauce.

Their hostess had rejoined them at the table and observed with one of her thin-lipped smiles that it would be a miracle if no change had taken place.

'Yes, I don't know how you stand it Mrs Drake,' said Scott Fenley, formal in his agitation. 'I mean, I realise that one would do anything to keep a roof over one's head these days, the place we're renting round the corner at the moment is far from perfect, but to have to live in such a grotesque way! Rabbit would die.'

'No, I wouldn't,' said Rabbit.

'You have been drinking, Rabbit,' whispered Scott Fenley. 'You know it makes you ill.'

'Only one martini, it's not so very much,' she said.

The next day, as Kate Drake was weeding the borders in the front garden, she saw Rabbit Fenley coming up the street with a face like a collapsed meringue. She was sobbing bitterly. Her black mascara had run and put both her cheeks in mourning.

'She's here, she's here,' wept Rabbit Fenley.

And behind her strode a woman who must have ransacked every skip in town for her outfit. The jacket and loose-flapping trousers bore unmistakeable stains of a pizza banquet.

'Help me,' wept Rabbit Fenley at the gate of number 22.

Kate Drake took her to the kitchen, away from the apparition, who was lounging menacingly against a lamppost on the other side of the road.

'She's put a curse on me,' wailed Rabbit Fenley.

'Now, now, you've had a shock,' said her rescuer. 'She won't stop long. She'll get tired of hanging about out there soon enough. Do you know her?'

This led to a fresh bout of tears.

'I don't, I don't. How would I know a creature like that? I'm married to someone in senior management. We don't meet people like that. I was on my way round, I needed company, and she just appeared. In the road. She said she was coming to claim her own. But' - there was a sudden shift in the villain's identity - 'it's not her really.

It's him, it's Scott. He's the one that's upset me. He made me have nightmares.'

'Oh, he did?'

'He *made* me. He kept on about - *that*.' Rabbit's eyes rolled wildly in the direction of the back garden. 'I had such terrible dreams and he wouldn't hold my hand. And the stairs creak so where we're living now, sometimes I think there's someone there. I can't go back to the house, I can't. What shall I do?'

Kate Drake went to the sitting room and looked through the window. The street was deserted. When she came back Rabbit Fenley had slumped forward and was lying with her head on the table and her hair trailing in the butter dish.

'Get up, Rabbit Fenley,' said Kate. 'The coast is clear. You're hardly in a fit condition to go anywhere but we'll drive to Port Meadow and take a walk.'

Rabbit Fenley stirred and sucked the butter from her hair. 'I can't go out there. *She's* out there.'

'There's no one out there. I've checked.'

Getting Rabbit Fenley to the door was like forcing a desperate animal from its lair. She shrank and hung back and whimpered and then, exhibiting a frenzied strength, ripped a wall socket from the wall as she was bundled out.

On the meadow the hawthorn was in bloom and a cuckoo sang cheerfully in the distance.

'Rabbit Fenley, it's spring,' said Kate Drake.

Rabbit, worn out by the tussle in the house, walked meekly beside her, eyes to the ground.

They drifted towards Wolvercote and came to a pub where the armchairs were plushy and the atmosphere discreet. A place for winding down. Kate ordered some sandwiches and a round of drinks, gin for herself and a brandy which she thought might help Rabbit Fenley to get a grip. But in the interval between choosing a table and sinking into a brocaded chair, Rabbit Fenley had dissolved in tears again.

'I thought he loved me but he doesn't. He called me his fluffy girl and said we'd have bunnies together. He scares me now. He makes me dream. And I hate that one in your garden. Last night I dreamt there was a tree growing out there and a face was in the leaves.'

'Rabbit - '

'Don't call me that. I've got a name.'

'What shall I call you, then?'

'Oh, it doesn't matter. Rabbit will do. I'm used to it.'

The sandwiches arrived, little slivers of tomato poking like tongues out of the tooth-white bread. Red as tongues, white as teeth, and Rabbit Fenley weeping, weeping, dripping the traces of her dark mascara over the polished table top. The room was painted in crimson and in cream.

'Blood and bone,' moaned the sorrowful one.

'Oh, this is outrageous. This is my day off. Pull yourself together,' snapped her companion, and Rabbit Fenley hiccuped and said, surprisingly, 'Well, he's dogshit.'

'I beg your pardon?'

'Scott. That describes him.' Rabbit began stuffing her mouth full of sandwiches. 'I'll never go back there now. No, no, I won't. You just watch me and see if I do go back.'

On the return journey across the meadow they found an early briar rose. In a thicket where kingcups had flourished not so long ago they saw a toad. A troupe of boys went swinging past in wet suits. By the water's edge the doughty stalwarts of a rowing school were muscling canoes about.

'You've got a spare room, haven't you?' said Rabbit Fenley.

'Well, you're forgetting. There's a problem with my house. A problem with the garden.'

'I'm not so worried about that any more. I think I got it out of my system in the pub, thank you. And in a way it's exciting, isn't it? It's very strange.' Then the eyelids started flickering and the eyes spilled over. 'You will help me, won't you?' said Rabbit Fenley. 'Don't turn me away.'

In tears she had a frail and haunted look, so wispy that a good strong gust would have finished her.

'I can't go back,' she said timidly. 'I did something this morning.'

'Meaning?'

'I sawed the corner cabinet in half. I took the big saw to it. He bought it in an auction, he was proud of it. If I went back now he might push me down the old stairs and my neck would break. Do you see? I can't go back.'

The car park was just off Walton Street. Rabbit Fenley brightened up as they skirted round town and she seemed almost happy. But at the corner of Baynard Way she took fright again in case the tattered woman was still about and threw her coat over her head, and once they'd stopped she scurried up the path of number 22 and made straight for the spare room. When Brad Drake got in he heard scrabbling noises aloft.

'Sounds like we might have a bird trapped up there, Kate,' he said. 'I'd better have a look.'

'It's Rabbit Fenley,' said Kate. 'She's moved into the spare room.'

'Rabbit Fenley has moved in?' He was staggered.

'Not for long, I hope. But she's in a bad way. I had to do something. She's leaving Scott.'

He sat down. 'Let's get this straight. Rabbit Fenley has left Scott Fenley and is scratching and squeaking in our spare room?'

'Yes.'

'She's taken up residence just like that and no one's bothered to ask for my opinion?'

'You weren't around or I would have.'

'And why is she leaving him?'

'She thinks he doesn't love her any more so she doesn't love him.'

'Well, I know we're short of money Kate, but I'm not sure that I want a paying guest.'

'She probably won't be paying. I doubt she has a penny to her name.'

'And why, if it's not too much to ask,' said he with a pointed smile, 'should we keep Rabbit Fenley?'

'Because she's left Scott.'

'Oh, we're going round in circles, aren't we?' he said fretfully. 'It's getting absurd. We can't collude with this, you know. Scott Fenley's a friend now.'

'He was. Maybe he won't want to be in future.'

'And Rabbit Fenley's as neurotic as they come. She'd never cope with our pal in the garden.'

'She sees it as a choice between the corpse and Scott Fenley,' said Kate. 'It seems she prefers the corpse.'

Her husband swigged a cup of tea and clicked his fingers tetchily. 'Look, I'm trying to be reasonable, Kate, but I've had a pig of a day, the bloody bursar's on about cost-cutting measures again, I'm tired, and I get home to find that you've turned the house into a no-hopers' refuge without so much as a by-your-leave, and when I ask a few perfectly straightforward questions all I get is cheap comments.'

'Well, you should have had the day I've had. I'd sooner do the midnight shift in a morgue than play nurse to Rabbit Fenley.'

'Yet you want her to live with us!' he said triumphantly. 'You don't even like her.'

'I don't like her, I don't hate her. I'm vaguely sorry for her. Beneath this cold exterior, you know, there beats a bleeding heart.' The lips were more string-like than ever.

'There's one thing about you that really gets me, Kate,' said Brad, staring her right between the eyes. 'It's the way you thin your lips out. It really pisses me off. You look like a public school headmistress gone to seed. Has anyone told you that before?'

'Oh, get stuffed.' She smashed a glass on the floor to add a touch of drama and, because she was exhausted by it all, snapped, 'you can take most of the blame for this on yourself. If you'd had a few more aspirations and hadn't settled for a lousy, bog-standard job, we'd have been better off and we wouldn't have had to go for a package that included a bag of bones out in the geranium bed. Which means that we wouldn't have come here in the first place and we'd never have met the Fenleys.'

He gave a slow grin. 'What about your own bog-standard job?'

'I'm doing very well, I'll have you know. Next year I'll be in charge of the workshop.'

'Ha, ha, big deal.'

'It's a bigger deal than the one you're on. All you're ever going to get is a curved spine and splitting headaches from the bloody cataloguing.'

There was a knock at the door.

'Answer that,' he shouted.

'Answer it yourself - if you can drag your beer gut that far.'

Another knock.

'Oh, I bet that's Don Giovanni come round, that'd be nice,' she exclaimed, and he growled, 'Yes, that's it. Flaunt your culture at me. A couple of months at art school ten years ago and you think you're on nodding terms with the great minds of the past.'

She wrenched the door open, crying back at him, 'I'm only doing this to get away from you.' She recognised the pizza-stained ensemble that stood outside immediately.

'I've come to collect my property,' said the woman. 'It's out in the garden.'

Rabbit Fenley's eyes appeared on the landing above.

'I was the lawful spouse,' said the assortment of rags, pushing her way through the hall and into the sitting room. 'I've waited long enough now. I'm here to claim my rights.'

'Is this another of your down-and-out buddies, Kate?' demanded Brad Drake, on his high horse behind the evening paper.

'I'm looking for a spade,' said the rags.

Rabbit Fenley started screaming on the landing upstairs. By the time Kate Drake had carried her down and swaddled her in a blanket, Mrs Sefton had found a spade and was already delving.

THE RECLUSE OF IFFLEY

MARGARET PELLING

Emma Curteys put another log on the fire. As she
pushed herself upright, there it was again – Aah!
– that sawing pain across her back that was as sure a sign
of cold weather as snow turning your feet numb. They'd
been mistaken to think spring was coming early, this first
night of Lent was as biting cold as midwinter. 'No soul
will be out willingly tonight who wants to live to see the
dawn, Sister,' she said.

The Bourdet girl merely sighed. Was she hankering
after being out, even in a world as cold as this one?
Foolish girl!

The lady's light was still burning when Emma and the
girl were ready to lie down to sleep, but that was nothing
new, the lady slept little. Did she sleep at all, what with
all the praying? Not that the likes of Emma Curteys was
exempt from praying, God help her. Oh, the torrents of
Our Fathers and Hail Marys in these last years. But those
weren't prayers, not real ones. There was only one real
prayer: *Lord, subdue this devil in me, preserve me from
these demons for pity's sake.*

They'd held off now a while, though, the demons.
Were they vanquished, dared she hope?

'Do you wish anything, my lady?' she said, as she
always did at the day's end.

'No, Emma, but I thank you for asking,' said the lady
in that slow, gentle voice of hers, as she always did. She

*Annora de Braose, daughter of marcher lord William de Braose who
fell foul of King John, and widow of Hugh de Mortimer, was enclosed
as an anchoress at St Mary's Church, Iffley, near Oxford, from 1232
until her death (probably in 1241). She is likely to have had servant
women, but nothing is known of them.*

had few wishes these days, but that was no reason not to ask her. It was the more reason to do so.

'Good night, then, my lady.' Emma yawned. Weather like this was wearying, what with going about the day's errands in a heavy mantle, as well as the baskets to carry. As she turned away from the lady, an icy blast slapped at her face. Holy Mary, the girl was at the door! 'Must you, Sister?'

Bourdet didn't answer, she just stood there, gazing out. She was busy with that communing of hers, that nightly succumbing to the embraces of Nature. Foolish, foolish girl! 'Yes, Sister,' she said at last, 'I must. Come and look, it's beautiful.'

The snow was falling fast now, and the rising wind blew stinging flakes against Emma's face. Beautiful, was it? Black, rather, as black as doom – too black even to make out the old yew tree, their closest neighbour. There were no lights showing over at the Hall. They themselves might be the only folk left alive in Christendom.

Bourdet's eyes were closed. Where was her mind? Not where her body was, that much was certain. It was off on the wind, flying to foreign lands she'd never see. What, what, was to be done about this girl? Couldn't Hamon and Matilda Bourdet have brought one of their other surplus plain daughters to serve here? God knew there were enough of them.

The girl opened her eyes. 'What was that?' she said.

'What was what, Sister?'

'That sound.'

'I heard no sound.'

'I did. Or, rather, I did *not*.'

'You talk in riddles, Sister.'

She frowned. 'I did hear something, only it was more the ghost of a sound. And now I hear that feeling in the air in the moments after a sound's died away. Listen, and you'll hear it too.'

Emma laughed, or tried to. Was there any limit to the girl's fancifulness? The only sound out there was the wind moaning around the high church tower, sounding too much like a lost soul. 'Shut the door,' she said, shivering, and turning back into the room, 'you'll let the Devil in.'

The instant those words were spoken, it was as if the snow were blowing deep into her vitals. But it was only a saying! Fat Joan, the reeve's wife, had said it a hundred times if she'd said it a dozen. Emma held out her hands to the flames, but the shivering wouldn't stop. Who was the fool now? The Evil One had never pranced around this dwelling on cold dark nights in a flourish of horns and forked tail. If he ever were to call, it would be on a bright summer day, looking docile and beguiling. Like a young girl.

Enough.

Bourdet joined Emma beside the fire but said nothing, just stared into the flames. Seeing castles and mountains in the flickering shapes and shadows, no doubt. Yes, Amice Bourdet had the wrong life in front of her, and she would suffer for it. Did the lady know this? She knew so much. But not everything, she didn't know everything. The lady didn't know why she, Emma, had selected this girl to help in the house when there'd been Eva Durandal with her red mane of hair and swan-necked Constance d'Eu to choose from too, each far better suited. Only God and the Devil knew why.

'If you heard anything just now, is it any wonder? People do hear things at night, even in a village. Animals are on the prowl, sometimes of the human kind, on their way to take fish out of the river where they shouldn't.'

The girl wrinkled her nose. 'I'm sure you are right, Sister,' she said quietly, and turned away to her bed.

Emma lay down and pulled the covers over her. 'Kyrie Eleison, Christe Eleison, Kyrie Eleison,' she said. It was always the last thing she said before sleep. To think that when she was young, she used to wonder whether there was any need – what offence had she committed today? Ah, was she ever that young?

'Amen,' said Bourdet.

Sleep began to draw itself up over Emma, like another covering. Just as it was reaching her eyes, the girl said, 'I hope it was an animal out there and not someone lost.'

'It was an animal. Now go to sleep.'

'Emma. Emma.'

Someone was calling from a long way off. Emma was running to them, but the faster she ran, the farther away drifted the someone, into a night so dark that –

'Emma!'

It took her some moments to come to her senses, to be aware that she was being called not by a phantom from a dream but by the lady. 'What is it, my lady?'

'There is someone at the door.'

'At the door? At *this* time?'

'Yes. Listen.'

She held her breath, and there it was, a faint knocking and then a scratching, as if someone or something was trying to claw through the door.

'Unbolt the door, Emma.'

'But my lady – '

'Emma, someone may be in need.'

The scratching again, this time fainter, as if strength had all but failed on the other side of that door. She looked across the room at the girl. Still sleeping, sleeping the sleep of the young. She gathered her robe about her. Nothing for it but to step over to the door.

She tried to open the door only a crack at first, but there was a weight pressing against it and it swung wide open in a flurry of snowflakes. Two cloaked people rolled across the threshold – they presumably *were* people, but they were so heavily muffled they could have been sacks of wheat. She must have exclaimed without knowing it, because in the next moment the house was full of voices:

'What is it, Sister?' drowsily from the bed in the corner.

'Bring them in, bring them in, the poor creatures,' from my lady.

And from the larger of the 'creatures', 'Oh, have mercy, have mercy!' A man. A young man.

The other one neither moved nor spoke. Was it dead?

'Get up from that bed and help me, Sister,' Emma began, but when she turned, there the girl already was, at her elbow, with a lighted rush dip.

'Bring them to the fire, quickly,' said my lady.

Getting the man to his knees wasn't easy, he was no lightweight. When they made to draw him nearer to the hearth, he said, 'No, I beg you, let me see to my sister, let me see if she lives.' He turned to his companion and began plucking at her garments. In an instant Bourdet was down beside him saying, 'Let me help,' and she it was who turned over the recumbent form and pulled aside its veil.

The face that the firelight showed was of such fairness that time wavered, dissolved, lost its meaning. How otherwise could a corporeal woman of fifty summers or so not know how she came to be on her knees, her hands clasped as if in prayer? 'Give me the light!' Emma's hands shook as she took the rushlight from Bourdet and held it close to the young woman's nose. The face was pale, oh so pale, and the eyes were fast shut, as if in their last sleep. But there was breathing: the rushlight's flame was flickering.

'How does she do?' said the lady.

'She is in this world still.' But how near the threshold?

'Thanks be to God,' said my lady, and 'Amen!' said the young man, the word having scarcely breath enough in it to make it leave his lips.

Too soon for thanks, too soon! 'Take her feet, Sister, while I take her shoulders, we must get her close to the fire.' Bourdet didn't need to be told to remove the young woman's fine shoes and begin chafing her feet, while Emma rubbed her icy hands. *Live, live, live,* pulsed in her mind in time with the rubbing. The young man found the strength to drag himself to the fire as they worked. He was shivering fit to shake loose the teeth in his head, but never mind the young man, there were young men to spare in this world.

The young woman gave a groan. As her eyes opened, Emma's fell shut for two heartbeats. *Now* God could be thanked.

'Ulfhild,' said the young man, slowly and distinctly, still shivering, 'Ulfhild.' Was he addressing her, or announcing her name to her in case the cold had frozen her memory? She stared at him for a moment. 'Æth-æthelmar,' she stammered. 'Are we alive?'

'We are,' he said. 'Thanks to these good ladies.' He turned towards the lady. 'We would not have disturbed you for the world, but – '

'Think nothing of it,' said the lady. 'Emma, Amice, some bread and broth for these poor souls.'

'See to it, Sister,' said Emma, 'give them all that's left in the pot.'

'Where are we?' said the one who had had Death hovering over her.

'You tell her,' said Emma to the young man, but not taking her eyes from this sister of his, unable to look anywhere but at her.

'Ulfhild, we are on holy ground, we are in an anchorhold. The lady anchoress has given us sanctuary.'

'Welcome to you both,' said the lady through the window of the chamber upon which this room abutted, that window so small, beside that door which was ever locked from this side, and to which there was but one key which hung from a hook on the wall above the door. Emma's chief duty in this place: to guard that key. To guard it better than she seemed to be guarding her eyes at this moment.

Oh Jesus and Mary, the demons were *not* vanquished. She was gazing at one.

'But I confess I know nothing of where we were a moment ago, outside these walls,' said the young man, accepting food from Bourdet, who was not guarding her own eyes as much as she ought as she offered him the bowl. 'I know only that there is a church to which this house clings,' he went on.

'A common perception,' said Emma, 'but you might be more correct if you said the church clings to this house.'

A house which now had a demon under its very roof. A demon which had come to tempt her, Emma Curteys, how could there be any doubt?

'Emma is very loyal but she has a tongue,' said the lady. 'Don't mind her. Our church stands in the FitzNiel manor of Iffley, near Oxford.'

'Near Oxford,' he repeated. 'Then we have not lost our way as much as I feared. We are on our way to Godstow, where I deliver my sister to the nunnery. Our horse shed a shoe in the woods and we were overtaken by the snowstorm. We had to leave the creature and try to find shelter. I hope he will be found and cared for.'

Bourdet was now supporting the young woman, 'Ulfhild,' as she sipped from a beaker. Had anything less like an Ulfhild's face ever been fashioned out of human clay? Who were these people, that they'd set out with only one horse between them, and seemingly without baggage? The man seemed in more than brotherly thrall to the young woman – a demon too, in a vile alliance with her to collect souls? Or was he a victim of hers? Perhaps she preyed indiscriminately. A young man there, an old woman here, and then such waverers as she might find in a houseful of nuns: it would be all the same to her. She, Emma, should have let her die!

The beds had to be given up to the 'guests', of course. For those whose home this was, it was a case of wrapping up in mantles and hunkering down by the fire for what remained of the night, but that was safer than to sleep and let these visitors sit up. By and by, a feeling grew in Emma, and hardened into certainty. Whoever they were giving house-room to tonight, their names were no more Æthelmar and Ulfhild than was hers. They wouldn't carry old names of this country, not with the world as it was now hanging about them, as their fine clothes showed.

Tomorrow morning they had to be away from here, before any wickedness infected the walls of this house. Otherwise she was damned.

Before Prime, Emma was at the door. The wind had dropped and the snow ceased falling, and the glow of dawn was in the sky.

'Ah, the storm has passed,' said the young man, from just behind her, making her start.

Emma took hold of his arm. 'Speak low, the lady will be at her devotions. The river is below us. Barges call here daily on their way to and from Oxford. I will go down in a moment and wait until one is in sight, and then I will return and summon you. You must wake your sister and be ready to leave instantly.'

Her words must have communicated much, for the young man recoiled slightly, blinking. He seemed to be debating whether to say anything, but she didn't want to hear anything he might have to say.

'Sister Amice,' she went on, addressing Bourdet, who began prodding the fire noticeably faster than she'd been doing, 'prepare food for these people's journey.'

'Oh no, please, Sisters,' said the young man, 'I know well that anchorholds have little to spare.'

Emma made a shrug do for an answer. Let them take every morsel in the house, if they would but go.

Bourdet found it necessary to come to the door before doing as she'd been bid. 'How beautiful the snow looks,' she said to the young man.

'You would think men had vanished from the earth,' he said.

'Yes! But look, you can see where a deer has gone down to the river – '

'Sister!' said Emma.

But Bourdet wasn't listening. Not to her. She was tilting her head to one side and she was frowning. 'Horses,' she said. 'There are horses coming.'

'What?' Emma returned to the door.

Bourdet was right. The sound of hooves was faint – muffled by the snow – but horses were indeed coming this way, many of them, and fast.

The young man's face had gone as white as the snow. 'Oh God help us,' he said, 'they are coming for us. They will kill me and take her back.'

'No, they will not,' said a voice which had not uttered this morning except to God: the lady's. 'Emma, unlock my door and let our visitors in.'

'Let them in? To the *cell*?' said Emma, and in her shock she must have sounded stupid, for the lady said, as sharply as she'd ever heard her speak, 'Yes, woman! Get them in here, quickly, quickly.'

Bourdet was the one who was quick. She shut and latched the house door, reached down the key to the cell door and had it open before Emma could blink. But to allow anyone into that cell but herself and Bourdet to see to the lady's needs was *unthinkable*. The young man must know this. He was looking at the door, his mouth open.

'Raise up your sister,' hissed Bourdet, giving the young man a push towards the bed – Emma's bed – in which the young woman lay, still fast asleep, 'and go in, now!'

The young man seemed to come to. The young woman stirred as he seized her in his arms but before she fully woke Bourdet had pushed them through the door, tossed their cloaks in after them, and re-locked the door.

Emma took a long breath. For the young man to be in there was bad, but for the young woman to be in there... No, no, no!

She hadn't drawn many more breaths before there was a knock at the house door, the loud rapid knock of a man accustomed to have doors opened to him. She adjusted her head-covering so that it fell more closely about her face and went to the door.

The man outside was of a size to fill the doorway and blot out the sunrise. He reeked of hard riding and horseflesh. Just beyond the precincts of the church there were more men, some mounted, some dismounted and holding horses' heads. Exactly how many was hard to see, though there must have been half a dozen, maybe more. One of the horses whinnied and was quieted by its rider.

'Good morning to you, sir,' she said, keeping her head bowed, as servants must do in houses of this nature, and speaking with the meek tones that had been hard to come by, because rarely practised. 'This is an early hour to consult the lady – '

'I've not come to take advice from the anchoress,' he cut in – not disrespectfully, but forthrightly nonetheless. 'I wish to have conversation with you, mistress. News finds its way to anchorholds, and it is news I seek.'

News that she could supply, no doubt. Wait: if this man was seeking the pair within, why not just tell him they were there? Ah, but how could she give 'Æthelmar' and 'Ulfhild' away without betraying the lady too, for giving them sanctuary? Oh, saints above!

'Sir, will you come in?' said Bourdet, her eyes all innocence. 'Sit down and warm yourself, take something to eat or drink.'

He shook his head. 'I thank you, but no. Mistresses, have either of you seen or heard anything in the night, anything at all which might have made you wonder if humankind was about?'

'This is a quiet village at nights, sir,' said Bourdet, looking at Emma in the way anyone would who was sure of confirmation.

Lord, Lord, her hands were tied! 'Last night was no exception,' said Emma, shrugging her shoulders.

'Do you seek someone – is there someone at large we should beware of?' said Bourdet, opening her eyes wider and sounding a touch breathless. She was good, that had to be granted. She was very good.

Just then there came a sound from the cell, as of a stool being kicked, or a weight falling from a table. The man's gaze flicked sideways, his eyebrows arching.

Something happened in Emma's head: it was like the roll of an internal drum. The one thing needful now was to protect the lady. She stepped quickly across to the cell window. 'Is there any assistance you need, my lady?' she called. At least the window cloth was fastened. All the man would see was the white cross on the black ground that was the lady's only device now.

But, if the man were to take a step to his left, he'd see something of great interest to him. He'd see a pair of too-pretty shoes. They were still on the floor by Emma's bed.

'No, I thank you,' came the lady's sweet, low voice, with never a waver. 'A clumsy moment with my Psalter, of no concern.'

Returning to the door, Emma fought the urge to nudge the shoes behind the bed. The movement could seem untoward. At the door, she stood where she might block the man's view, please God.

'The lady's fingers will be cold,' Bourdet murmured, with nothing in her voice but devotion and reverence. She had seen the shoes, she must have.

'Indeed,' said the man, adjusting his sword belt. He was not much interested in the discomforts suffered by anchoresses. 'Now, as to the people we seek, there are two of them, a man named Ravenot, Amaury Ravenot, and a woman whose name I will not reveal. They are each young. They must be close by, we found their horse just now in the woods.'

'They've not been here,' said Emma. 'As you see, the only prints – human prints – in the snow are yours.'

'They could have come this way before the snow began to fall, or before it was thick.'

'If they did, they did so silently, like the deer.' She added another shrug of the shoulders for good measure. 'Ask at the Hall. They have sharp eyes and ears there.'

The man's eyes narrowed. He looked down at the ground for a moment, frowning and blowing a long breath out from between his teeth. The air from inside him turned into cloud as it met the chill air outside him. Then he looked up. 'Very well. If you do hear or see anything, in the coming days – discarded food, remains of a fire – tell the bailiff, tell the reeve, tell the priest – tell the first man with any authority here whom you can find.'

'Oh we will, sir, we will,' said the girl, round-eyed. 'But are they a danger, these people?'

'Only to themselves,' he growled, and turned away. 'We go on!' he shouted to the men waiting for him. As he strode off toward them, a horse whinnied again, and those who had dismounted swung themselves back into their saddles.

Emma retreated into the house. As the sounds of a body of mounted men grew fainter, she leaned against a bench. She was shaking, only it was as if she were outside herself watching herself shaking: how could that be? Bourdet remained by the door, her head turned toward the direction which the horsemen must be taking.

'Emma, Amice,' called the lady in a low voice, pulling aside her window covering, 'is it safe?'

'They've not gone far as yet,' murmured Bourdet. 'They've gone over to the Hall.'

'Then our guests will remain with me a while longer.'

The young man's face appeared at the window. 'Thank you sisters, thank you from the bottom of our hearts,' he said. His voice was a broken thing, the voice of a man much older.

'We will never let them take you, Master Ravenot,' said Bourdet, dropping her gaze. Well might she do so; her face was glowing.

Then the young woman appeared, 'Ulfhild'. Who was she, *what* was she, that the man who'd been here couldn't divulge her name? 'We owe our lives to you,' she said, simply. To see her there, her face framed by the window: it was enough to make Emma's entrails wind themselves around her heart, for that was how it felt. It was not that the young woman's gaze had force – no, it was full of mildness. Oh, this was a demon indeed!

'It's the lady whom you owe your lives to,' said Emma, her voice sounding rough and brusque in her ears. Yes, this one was a demon. What had happened just now was very plain: she had used the lady's goodness for her own ends. 'You'll be wanting some food. Excuse me,' Emma went on, turning away.

How long would they be here? Could they be got rid of by nightfall?

They were not gone by nightfall. The men who were seeking them went away only when the light was fast fading, having left no person of any wit in the village unquestioned and a good many fools besides. The man who had knocked at the door was right: news travels fast to anchorholds, and that day, the gossips came flocking like the crows which cawed in the trees around the church. The lady kept her windows closely covered; she was not one for idle talk, and her Rule would not encourage her to be indulging in speculation about the reasons why a young man and a young woman might go into hiding. Especially when the hiding place was the lady's cell. The most outlandish chatter was from Agnes the miller's wife and her eldest girl, Edith with the withered arm. They hurried in together, full of: 'She'll be the daughter of the King of Bohemia on her way to marry King Henry and she's been carried off by a Templar!'

'Is Iffley on the road from Bohemia to Canterbury? I think not,' said Emma. It was what they'd expect from dour Sister Emma, and all had to be as expected. After this torment was over – and it *would* be over, she *would* resist – she'd make a confession to the priest and this time tell the truth.

'Oh, but he's taking her to Ireland, the Templar!' Agnes chirped.

'He'll find King Henry has ships which can follow across a narrow sea.' Yes, confession was the only way. Otherwise the load of festering thoughts in her heart would drag her down on the sure and certain day of her death to the bottommost pit of Hell.

'They say he's six and a half feet tall with hair that shines like gold,' said Edith, her eyes as wide as her squint would allow. At this, the Bourdet girl looked up for a moment from stirring the pot.

Had the horsemen's leader said at the mill what the male fugitive looked like, or had sad silly Edith decided it for herself? She wasn't wide of the mark. An inch or two shorter and hair with more brown in it than gold, perhaps, but she'd know the man if the single wall separating him from her were suddenly to crumble.

Even the bridge-hermit left off his surveillance of the causeways for an hour to bring them half a dozen skinned rabbit whelps and warm himself at the fire. 'They'll be seeking a girl who doesn't want to be married, poor soul,' he said, crouching low over the fire and rubbing his hands. His robe, as it warmed, gave off a fleshy scent like a dog's.

'I'm surprised at you, Brother Ralph,' said Emma, 'spreading tales that are none of our business.'

'Sister Emma, you are the least curious person in the world. You are a marvel of continence.' He grinned as he looked up at her, showing his few remaining teeth.

Continence? Yes, she was continent. She had turned away from temptation – thus far. *Lead us not into temptation.* The number of times she'd said that, yet still, *still...*

There was a possibility, of course. A possibility so dire that her mind fled from it like a sparrow from a hawk: she would not, could not, let it take words.

When the last gossip had gone they let the fugitives out of the lady's cell. The young man was for leaving straight after supper, saying they'd journey by night, but the lady wouldn't hear of it. And so that night the young woman had Emma's bed again. The young man refused to deprive Bourdet a second night, and so it was Emma and he who spent the night in cloaks by the fire. When others were asleep, Emma said, 'You've overheard the stories today. Tell me the truth Master Ravenot, you owe us that.'

The young man sighed, then began speaking. In a low voice, he told a tale which contained something of the day's stories patched into it, but which in its whole was both more and less than those stories. He was squire to the young woman's father, and he was helping her escape a marriage hateful to her – a marriage which was due to have taken place that day. The bridegroom was not the King, and the bride was not a daughter of one, but the parties were sufficiently high in the land – and from sufficiently closer than Bohemia – that Ravenot, too, would not give names.

'What are you to her?' said Emma.

He sighed more deeply. 'A friend,' he murmured. 'Nothing more. Godstow nunnery is truth. She goes there willingly. She loves no man and never will.'

Loves no man and never will. Words to make a heart beat faster around this fire: too fast, and with no more hope of stopping than of the sun rising at midnight. She had to resist the demon, resist!

'What will you do then, Master Ravenot?' said Bourdet. So she wasn't asleep.

He shrugged. 'I do not know, Sister Amice. Become a Templar, perhaps, and give a little more truth to what the gossips were saying today. Or perhaps not.'

In other words, he didn't care. Was he then, like the lady, being used?

'Listen,' said Emma, leaning closer to him, 'those men today will have set up the hue and cry. They'll be looking for her at all the nunneries in these parts, and the walls of those houses may not be thick enough to keep them out and her in.'

He looked at her, his eyebrows arched.

'Tomorrow, early, take her down river to Henley, where the cogs from Flanders land. Contrive a passage on one of those ships. There are nunneries in Flanders and France, and Templar houses too. Whatever you do, go far away from here.'

Tomorrow, early, take her to the ends of the earth.

It was not to be. Not the next day, nor the next, nor the next. Not only were there fresh falls of snow each night and much of the days as well, but the men searching for the runaways were still in the neighbourhood, scouring each village. They were reported as far as Abingdon and Wallingford and up to Woodstock.

Ravenot and the young woman left the cell whenever it was safe, to allow the lady some solitude. Bourdet took it upon herself to guard the house door – not a task so arduous that it hindered her in commiserating with Ravenot for being cooped up so.

The young woman sat reading books the lady gave her. Emma spoke to her no more than was necessary, and when she did so, by a mighty effort of will it was with that gruff, brusque voice.

'I am sorry to be in your way, Sister Emma,' said the young woman at last, when Emma was sweeping the floor around her. 'I know we are a great disturbance and you wish us gone,' she went on. To that, it was impossible to say a word. Emma swept on, keeping her head down. The broom took it upon itself to bang against the table legs. 'And so please let me make recompense by helping with the work of the house.' The young woman put the book aside and rose.

'Oh – no – how can you think,' began Emma, but the lady was appealed to.

'Why, yes, we thank you,' said the lady. 'Not for recompense, though. You give your help as a gift, which we freely accept.'

There was no way around it. Smooth white hands which could never have touched a cooking pot or a wash tub came to be at work alongside Emma's rough red ones, and once the two pairs of hands chanced to brush against one another in the tub. The young woman looked up and smiled, and blood-boiling fire shot through Emma. She made her face like stone. How much longer, dear God?

'Sister Emma, have you been with the lady since she became a recluse?' said the young woman one day before Vespers when they were preparing the lady's meal.

'I've been with the lady all my life,' said Emma. 'My father was high in her father's service. There is no time when I have not been with the lady.' God forgive her the lie, if he didn't forgive her much else. Was this – weakness – of hers a punishment for pretending loyalty to the old king when the lady fled with her father and mother to Ireland, and for skulking away the years of the lady's imprisonment with relatives in York? She was never beset by it before that dreadful time.

Emma's hands shook as she ladled pottage into a bowl. She had spoken a shade less abruptly just now, she must be on her guard.

The lady invited the young woman to sit with her after her meal. While Emma cleared the dishes and tidied, the young woman began to speak to the lady: 'I can think of no better thing on this earth,' she said, 'than to live enclosed, as you do.' There was a catch in her voice. What a dissembler she was!

The lady stayed for some moments, head bowed, hands clasped in her lap. Then she said, 'When I entered this cell, that grave in the corner had already been dug for me. Psalms from the Office of the Dead were sung and dust was sprinkled over me. Do you understand what that means?'

The young woman said without a pause, 'Yes, I do. It is no longer you who live but Christ who lives in you. Oh, how I long to die to this world!'

Again, the lady was silent for some moments. 'To die once might not be enough. A sister of mine has been enclosed near Canterbury since perhaps before you were born. She has lost count of the number of times she has found herself to be still living, and challenged to die yet again.'

'This life is not easy, I know,' said the young woman, looking down.

The lady touched her hand. She said, her voice kind, 'My sister has also lost count of the number of times that Christ has carried her through, as He carries us all.'

Emma left them. Oh, if the lady only knew! This 'Ulfhild' was aptly named, after all. She might have the look of a lamb, but inside that tender breast beat the heart of a wolf.

After this the young woman said little and her eyes looked inward, but demons could watch you without seeming to look, they could watch you all the better. Emma's own eyes were all but tight shut, but she knew the young woman was watching her – watching her every waking moment, and the sleeping moments too. The young woman was watching her even when she was out collecting supplies for the household.

That dire possibility of days ago began to clothe itself in words, twist and turn as she would to keep them away. What if – what if a demon had long ago entered into *her*, Emma Curteys? What if the demons who came at her were merely like answering like?

The day of her customary call on Fat Joan for barley and peas, she was much delayed at the reeve's house. 'Come in, come in, good Sister Emma, sit you down and take a cup of ale,' cried Joan, and her broad rosy face with its many chins widened into a beaming smile. To smile back was a trial, and two beakers apiece weren't enough for Joan to impart how the midwife didn't know her business, Peter Hayward's wife was not four weeks from her term, she was two weeks, and that Henry Smith's mother, poor old soul, had rallied again, but the priest's last visit to her would happen before May was out, 'I'll stake my own soul on it.'

'Have you heard tell if those two young fugitives have been found yet?' said Emma. Why, why in the world, did she ask that?

'What, the squire and his lord's girl? I've heard they've been sighted in more places than they could ever have been in unless they've got wings. Maybe half a dozen pairs of youngsters are abroad, maybe it's the season for them, like the wildfowl returning.' Joan laughed, and slapped her knee. 'Good luck to them, I say. If they've any sense, they'll have flown far away by now.' She leaned forward. 'The men who came searching have gone back to their lord with their tails between their legs, I hear. Best place for 'em.' She laughed again, loud and long.

Had they, indeed. And the snow was melting and the weather getting warmer. Perhaps there was a chance.

When she returned, a plan of escape was being born. The news that the search seemed to have been given up brought it forth: 'It will be tomorrow, early,' said Ravenot. 'We will make our way to Oxford and be at East

Gate ready to slip in with the first market-goers of the day. We'll lose ourselves in the town until we can take a boat down river. We'll be less likely to be noticed in the press of people in Oxford than if we embark here.' He seemed tense, but was that surprising? The venture was not without risk.

Bourdet, her eyes cast down, was already preparing food for them to take.

That evening, Bourdet did not catch Emma's eye, and she did not catch Bourdet's. Tomorrow, the birds which had roosted with them would fly, and they would never see them again. She could almost find it in her to feel sorry for Bourdet, if she herself had not had the steadily growing feeling that she did indeed harbour a demon. Why else should there be this strange sensation in her at the prospect of the young woman's finally going? It was as if her heart were weeping.

Goodbyes were made before they all settled to sleep. The departure was to be made with no fuss, long before Prime. When Emma and Bourdet roused themselves, it would be as if the visitors had never been.

The young woman insisted on Emma's taking her bed once more. It must have been the unaccustomed luxury after nights of making shift, because against all the odds Emma slept so heavily that she woke only when the house door was opened and then closed.

The darkness was still thick and black. She waited, head beneath the covers, until she heard Bourdet rise and stir the fire. Five heartbeats later, she sat up.

'Good morning, Sister,' said – *not* Bourdet.

Emma froze in the act of putting a foot to the floor. It was the young woman who had greeted her. She leaped to her feet, looked all around. Had the young woman and Ravenot not gone yet? But she had heard them leave!

She must have looked stupefied, her mouth hanging open, for the young woman smiled and murmured, 'All is well, Sister. The two who wanted to go have gone, the one who wanted to stay has stayed.'

'But – how – '

She came forward and took Emma's unresisting hands. 'Forgive me, Sister. This plan has been brewing in my mind, but it was not until yesterday, when you were out and the lady was sleeping, that I disclosed it to the others. Sister Amice said yes immediately.'

'And Master Ravenot?' Emma choked out the words.

The young woman looked aside for a moment. 'When Amaury saw that we were set on this scheme, he was persuaded,' she said quietly. Then she looked full at Emma. 'Very few have seen Amice Bourdet, really looked at her. It fell to her to remain here all day while you were out and about, as the Rule says. She and I are of a size, and with the veil pulled well down I shall pass for her. Sister Emma, I believe God wants this, He has brought me here and taken Amice away. She was not meant for this life.' She looked at Emma, so wanting her approval, still clinging to her hands. 'I shall be a good worker in the house, I promise,' she said softly.

Emma looked at her. It was all she could do. Mind and will would not function.

'Emma, would you please bring me a light, my candle has gone out,' came the lady's voice.

It was the voice the lady used for Bourdet, not for herself. But it couldn't be.

The young woman, with no hesitation, lit a rush dip and took it to the cell window.

The window cloth was pushed aside. 'I have been thanking God this morning for the gift of good health, especially where the ears are concerned,' said the lady as she held her candle to the window. 'I have seldom needed so little sleep nor heard so well as in this last day or so.'

'May God be praised,' said Emma's lips. Her body moved toward the fire and began tending it, though it needed no attention, this other one had made it burn brightly.

'So your name is Emma,' she found words to say, when the lady's window was closed again.

'Yes,' said the young woman, smiling. 'I am Emma. Like you.'

A LITTLE PERSISTENCE

JANE GORDON-CUMMING

Peggy Hardwick slipped into the garden by the back gate, as she so often had when Mr Crowmarsh was alive. She took a couple of the rosemary cuttings he had promised her, and rescued a pair of rusting secateurs from their grave in the rose garden. Soon there would be children here again, chasing each other round the old apple trees and making dens in the overgrown shrubbery. It would be good to see a family enjoying this old North Oxford garden, and that would have to be some compensation for the loss of her friend.

She moved gently through the long grass of the orchard, remembering how they had plotted their last campaign here. Hugh Crowmarsh had been chairman of the local amenity society, and a vigorous opponent of all modern development. His elegantly worded letters to the City Council had somehow always contrived to make the opposing view seem trivial and mercenary, and it was largely due to him that this part of Oxford had remained virtually free of intrusive new buildings. If, by any chance, he failed to convince them the first time, Mr Crowmarsh had the added gift of perseverance. 'A little persistence,' he used to say, 'nearly always ends in triumph.'

Peggy had been secretary of the society, curbing the worst excesses of the old man's eccentricity and seeing to such mundane matters as stamps and postcodes. They had made a good team. She missed him badly.

Since his death, the house had lain empty. Wisteria stretched long fronds unchecked up into the guttering. The fine grass on the old tennis court grew long and straight, while the bindweed rejoiced in its opportunity to embrace the roses, and opened its own white flowers to rival theirs.

Peggy made no attempt to interfere with this paradise. The pleasure of reclamation must be left to the new owners. She let herself out of the back gate and slipped away.

Kevin Bucknell had come through the front. He stepped carefully into the garden, disentangling a bramble from the sleeve of his light grey suit, unhooking his tie from a rose thorn. He took out a long tape and measured the house in metres and the garden in fractions of a hectare. Mr Crowmarsh's estate had been left to his sons, Julian and Christopher, and their solicitors had placed the property in the hands of an estate agent.

Despite the wet hem of his smart trousers and the damp leaves clinging to his shiny black shoes, Kevin smiled happily as he filled in his notebook and snapped the front of the house with his digital camera. The property had a substantial amount of land, and there would be room for three building plots without crowding. It should fetch a good seven figures at auction - a nice little sum each for Julian and Christopher, and a tidy commission for his firm.

Julian, in his Chelsea flat, put the dull-looking envelope to one side. He was telling his companion about a visit he had paid to a stately home the day before in his capacity as an inspector of historic buildings.

'Just imagine, Bernard - an absolute gem of Victorian gothic, and they'd put in plastic-framed windows! Would you believe the insensitivity of it?'

Bernard tutted sympathetically, and Julian, gratified, turned to the Sotheby's catalogue that had come in the same post. He leafed through it wistfully. There was some really nice stuff coming up that he couldn't possibly afford to bid for.

The letter telling him that his father's property in Oxford, divided into four lots, should bring him a half-share in a very sizeable sum, was welcome news indeed.

Christopher Crowmarsh's letter was opened by his wife, Monica. He was a busy man, after all, so she felt it was reasonable to save him the trouble of slitting envelopes. Besides, it was from his solicitors, and she wanted to know what it said.

Christopher, peacefully reading the Guardian, was startled by her shriek of delight. 'Oh, that's wonderful! Now we can afford to send Tarquin to public school! Who would have thought that ramshackle old place was worth so much?'

When Christopher was finally able to take the letter and see the figure for himself, he agreed it was a surprising amount. With that sort of money he would have preferred to buy a bigger house, a family place with a large garden. He looked across at Tarquin, carefully dividing his muesli into piles of raisins and nuts and oatflakes along the edge of his bowl, and tried to persuade himself that his son was worth educating to the tune of all those thousands of pounds.

When Peggy Hardwick saw the estate agents' board, she couldn't believe her eyes. There must be some mistake. She went into the garden and found where Kevin's firm had driven wooden stakes into the ground to mark off the different building plots: one row along the raspberry bed, another among the delphiniums and one right across the tennis court. What was left of the garden would be shadowed by the old house in the morning and the new ones in the evening.

The real irony was that this was just the sort of development Mr Crowmarsh would have opposed most vigorously. 'Sheer barbarism!' she could hear him saying. 'We must protest in the strongest terms.'

She wrote to the planning committee, but the reply she received was unencouraging. It spoke of 'sensitive development' and 'unobtrusive infilling' and the constraints of the Local Plan. As a last resort, she wondered whether to write to Mr Crowmarsh's sons. Christopher was a businessman up north - not much point appealing to him. But wasn't the elder brother something to do with historic buildings? She wrote, care of the solicitors, explaining that she was an old friend of his father's, and how much he would have disapproved of his garden being sold off for development.

But Julian had spent a lifetime trying to disassociate himself from his father's eccentric opinions, and saw no reason to respect them any more now that he was dead. He wrote Mrs Hardwick off as a local busybody and did not reply to the letter.

As the date of the auction drew nearer, Christopher Crowmarsh felt a great desire to see his old home once more before it was sold.

Monica tried to dissuade him. 'What do you want to go down there again for? Surely you saw it at the funeral?'

'Yes, but not the garden. It was pouring with rain that day. I was so happy there. I just want to see it once more.'

Monica didn't say anything about happiness. She was happy, with her child and her house and Christopher doing so well with his computer firm. She didn't want him to make this nostalgic trip south.

'A hotel in Oxford for the night won't be cheap,' she said.

'Cheaper than public school,' said Christopher.

By July the garden had become a battlefield. Columbine and honeysuckle chased each other round the pergola, ivy fought clematis for possession of the wall, while couch-grass chased calendula across the rockery and out on to the lawn.

It was something of a shock to Christopher. Could these really be the neat grass paths of his mother's beloved rose garden, now indistinguishable from the weeds in the beds? Were these spiky little bushes the box hedge that had formed such an exciting maze for them as children? And wasn't this where he had kissed Anne Horley, in the dark sweet-smelling passage between the wall and the bay-tree? There wasn't a passage any more. The bay-tree pressed against the wall as closely as he had pressed against Anne that day.

Mrs Hardwick had also slipped into the garden to say goodbye. They came face to face among the raspberries and apologised, recognising each other from the funeral. She was embarrassed at being caught trespassing, he at being caught with his memories.

'It's hard to let go of a place one grew up in,' he said. 'Every corner of this garden is so much part of my childhood. I had a wonderful secret den under that laurel bush. Oh well! Some other child will discover it and enjoy it just as much, I dare say.'

'I don't think so,' said Mrs Hardwick, seeing him point to the heart of the area allocated to Lot Number Two.

'No?' He was surprised at the sharpness of her voice.

'That is where one of the new houses is going to be.'

'What new houses?'

They stared at each other in mutual incomprehension.

'Surely you knew the garden was being sold off for building land?'

Christopher slowly shook his head. Come to think of it he had never read that letter properly. Monica had been so preoccupied with the money.

'They plan three building plots,' said Mrs Hardwick, watching him, 'with separate access from the road. Your laurel bush will go, of course, and the tennis court, and the rose garden...'

'Oh no!' said Christopher. 'They can't do that!'

Peggy's heart bounded with hope. 'You'll stop the sale then - despite the money?'

'I had no idea they meant to break up the garden! There's no question... The money? Why, would it be a lot less, do you think?'

'About half as much,' said Mrs Hardwick, who'd made a point of finding out.

Christopher gazed at her, seeing not her face but Monica's, and listening to Monica's reaction on being told that Tarquin was not to go to public school after all, just because his father did not want to spoil a garden.

'I can't do it,' he groaned. 'I can't stop the sale.'

Peggy was surprised. Seeing him at close quarters she no longer thought he was the mercenary type.

'Surely you wouldn't want to see all this destroyed - the whole of your childhood - for the sake of a few thousand pounds?'

He looked round him like a trapped animal. If it was impossible to explain to Monica why he must keep the garden, it was impossible to tell this woman why he could not.

'Sometimes,' he said, 'one can't have just what one wants.'

'Your father used to say,' said Mrs Hardwick softly, 'that you can always get something you *really* want. It just takes a little persistence.'

'Yes,' smiled Christopher. 'He said that to me when I failed to make the cricket team the first time. He was right, too. I got in next year.'

That night in his hotel bed, Christopher found it hard to sleep. He remembered how Mrs Hardwick had told him she'd written to Julian about the garden. That was a laugh! Although he might have inherited his father's appreciation of the aesthetic, the beautiful things Julian liked were the kind one had to pay for. Christopher could well imagine his reaction to being asked to forgo a six-figure sum for such a cause.

It was funny, really. Julian spent his life preserving historic buildings, fighting applications to make the most trivial alterations, yet when it came to his own home...

What if Max Westwell got to hear of it? Max was an old school friend of theirs who worked for a satirical magazine. Julian often passed him juicy titbits about members of the aristocracy vandalising their stately homes. This was just the sort of thing he would revel in - a prominent conservationist inherits a notable Oxford garden and sells it off for building plots!

Christopher sat up in bed. If such a thing *were* to be published, it would make Julian a laughing-stock among everyone he respected. The threat of publication would be enough to make him veto the sale.

He lay down again. He could hardly tell Max himself, and no one else was likely to tip him off. He drifted off to sleep, cutting letters out of an imaginary copy of *Country Life* to form the words 'vandalism' and 'amenity'. He dreamed that Mrs Hardwick was trying to serve a ball over to him on the waist-high grass of the tennis court, and saying 'a little persistence...'. When he woke, the solution was clear.

The letter Max Westwell read was not cut out of *Country Life*, but written in Peggy Hardwick's clear hand. He might be interested to know that Julian Crowmarsh, well known for his work in the conservation of ancient buildings, had no compunction about destroying a Victorian garden in favour of a quick buck.

Max chuckled. If this was true it would make a great item for the Diary column. He rang Julian Crowmarsh.

Julian could hardly contain his anger. He blustered and talked heatedly about interference and nosey parkers. Max had been prepared to hear it was all a mistake, but Julian's tone made him think there might be some truth in it. He was convinced when Julian said, 'You won't publish this, will you? Come on, Max - for the sake of the old school tie!'

'I'm sorry, old boy, but you must agree that it's too good a story to miss. Someone else'll only print it if I don't - assuming it's true, of course.'

'Well it's *not* true!' snapped Julian. 'The garden isn't going for building land at all. It'll be sold as one lot with the house. Make a story of that!'

Max tried to keep the disappointment out of his voice, as he assured Julian that in that case, there would of course be no story.

Julian relieved his feelings by throwing the Sotheby's catalogue in the bin. He wondered what Christopher and Monica would say when they heard that he was refusing to let the garden be sold separately. It would be wisest to inform them through the solicitors, he felt. Otherwise there might be an unpleasant scene.

Monica couldn't believe her eyes when she saw the letter. That wretch, Julian, and his silly principles! Why, they'd only get half the money now! It was poor little Tarquin she felt sorry for...

Christopher poured her a cup of tea to calm her down. 'Never mind,' he said. 'If the house is only worth half as much, we'll be able to buy Julian's share and move into it ourselves.'

Peggy Hardwick loved autumn bonfires. She loved the smell, and the feeling of clearing away dead things. There was a lot to clear in this garden, but the new owners were only too grateful for her offer of help. She was careful not to destroy anything that might still flower, and her pruning was perhaps over-cautious, but when one had so nearly lost the whole...

She had enjoyed trimming the box hedges, though. Now they were a child-sized maze again, and she looked forward to watching little Tarquin running round them. Oh dear, this was a stubborn bramble. Even the tiny ones seemed to cling. There, out at last! Wonderful what a little persistence could do.

A VERY MODERN AFFAIR

ANGELA CECIL-REID

Alison peered at the steaming pile on the doormat. That bloody cat. It never knew when it had eaten enough. She sighed and headed for the kitchen roll. Finished. She picked up a newspaper from the recycling basket. Pausing at the utility room window, she looked out across the garden towards the row of lime trees fringing Charlbury Road. Usually she loved this time of the morning when the sturdy Victorian houses breathed a collective sigh of relief at the return of peace after the morning rush. But not today.

She had only been up for an hour and already she had had to turn the house upside down searching for Richard's passport. In the end she had found it, one corner slightly chewed, in Chocolate's basket. She glanced across at the four-month-old Labrador. He was curled up with Atlas, the largest ginger cat in the world. Both were sound asleep, and both looked deliciously cuddly and innocent of all charges. Appearances certainly could be deceptive.

Then there had been the phone call from Rebecca. Could she wrap up Chessington and send him this very morning, by recorded delivery, up to Newcastle?

'But darling, I've no idea where he is. You packed him away when you decided that going to university meant putting away childish things.'

'Mum, this is an EMERGENCY. If I don't have him I'll fail my exams. I won't make it into the second year. Please Mum...'

Alison had sighed as she realised a good part of her morning would be taken up with finding, packing and despatching the bear. She tried to ignore the thought that slipped into the back of her mind - so what else had she been planning to do with it?

Just as she had kissed a tight-lipped Richard goodbye, wished him a speedy trip to Paris and was heading upstairs to look for Chessington, the phone had rung again. This time it was James. As she never heard from him unless there was a disaster, she couldn't help a flicker of dread as she waited for him to get past the preliminaries.

'Hi Mum, how you doing?'

'Fine, darling. What's wrong?'

'What d'you mean, wrong?' The voice was irritated, defensive.

Alison was immediately contrite. 'Sorry. It's good to hear from you. How are the finals going? Are we seeing you soon?'

'Not sure, Mum. I've had this great idea. I think I should broaden my mind this summer. Do a bit of travelling. Maybe join a charity project. Would look good on my CV. But...' His voice trailed away.

Alison took pity on him. 'But you're short of money?'

His voice was suddenly warm, encouraging, grateful - deliberately irresistible. 'I'll pay you back. Just as soon as I've got a job. Honest. Mum, you're a real star.'

Alison sighed again, and realised that currently her whole life seemed to be one long sigh. 'How much do you need?'

Alison peered at the cat vomit. She wished it wasn't still steaming. That made it worse somehow. She unfolded the newspaper and was about to use it to scoop up the mess when a headline caught her eye: '*When Monogamy Becomes Monotony.*'

Intrigued, she read on. '*Four out of five married people are having an affair, according to recent research which looked at the effects of the internet on fidelity. Online dating has reached new heights as more and more sites are targeting dissatisfied husbands and wives with a range of services specifically designed for married people who want to walk on the wild side. Sites such as www.a-bit-on-the-side.com and www.threes-company. co.uk are attracting large numbers of visitors, with men outnumbering women by four to one.'*

Alison dealt with the cat vomit and binned the soiled paper. What a ridiculous article, she thought as she set about the search for Chessington. If it were in any way true, it would mean that in this street alone more than three-quarters of the people she knew would be having an affair. She tried to imagine the Westcotts who lived opposite indulging in a cyber-romance. Surely Rupert, with his wide baby-blue eyes, and the gorgeously curvy Samantha had more than enough going for them without the need for external interests.

So maybe Marjory and John Rutherwood, who lived next door in Number 59, were contenders? But as hard as she tried she just couldn't see it. It was impossible to visualise balding John, with his ever-widening girth, and Marjory, with her sensible shoes, tweed skirts and varicose veins, at the heart of a lust-driven marital drama.

At last Chessington was unearthed from a box in the attic, and the house returned to its naturally immaculate state. Alison headed towards the study armed with a cup of coffee and a piece of chocolate cake; she could always return to the cabbage and grapefruit diet tomorrow. She would just check her email and then transfer the money to James's gaping hole of an account.

The emails didn't take long. There was one from Amazon saying she would be pleased to know her order had been despatched. She sighed yet again, thinking that it would probably take more than reading *Ten Simple Steps to Conquer the Menopause* or *So the Birds Have Flown – Now What?* to solve her problems.

There was also an email from Richard at the airport saying his plane was on time and he was sorry about the passport drama; he really hadn't meant to lose his temper, it was just the wretched cold he seemed to be coming down with. He would bring her back something wonderful from Paris, and he'd see her in time for dinner on Friday.

Alright for some, thought Alison, gazing at the blanks on the calendar in front of her. The most exciting thing she had to look forward to this week was her Pilates class on Wednesday.

She found herself wondering, as she often did, if Richard thought about her when he was on one of his trips? Or was he too involved with the meetings, the smart hotels and the exotic locations? There were usually few phone calls and only the odd email to remind each of the other's existence. Richard was actually the perfect candidate for an extra-marital affair. She had once tackled him on the subject after a particularly long trip to Thailand. He had looked at her with exhausted eyes.

'You are joking aren't you? I race from one meeting to the next and hardly know whether it's day or night. I don't have time to breathe let alone meet anyone.'

Then he had slept virtually all weekend. That had been the first time she had been aware of the grey streaks in his chestnut hair, and the wrinkles round the sea-green eyes she had fallen in love with so many years before.

Alison dealt with the money transfer and was about to log off when unbidden into her mind leapt the words, *when monogamy becomes monotony*.

Just a brief look, she thought, could do no harm. No harm at all. And as for the old saying about curiosity and cats, she glanced through to the kitchen, Atlas was the most curious, as well as the greediest, cat she had ever been acquainted with, and he was showing no signs of impending death – unfortunately, bearing in mind his recent gift to her on the doormat.

A Google search on adultery duly brought up a list of sites, of which two were already familiar. Alison keyed in www.a-bit-on-the-side.com and her screen was instantly alive with cartoons of naked couples holding hands and in some cases holding rather a lot more. More brothel than romance there, she thought, and quickly tapped in www. threes-company.co.uk

This time the screen was a reassuring shade of sky-blue, overlaid with dark blue silhouettes of bluebells and flying doves. Alison took a deep breath and clicked on *Enter the Site*.

The home page assured her that this was the site for people who already had a good marriage, but who believed an essential ingredient was now missing from their lives. Maybe they needed friendship, or perhaps a little passion? The site was utterly discreet and couples would have complete control – they might never even meet, and prefer to remain in a cyber-romance, never even knowing who the other truly was, or they might choose to walk in a park holding hands – the decision was theirs. At the bottom of the page, a button flashed at her - *Register Now*.

Alison stood up and returned to the window. A crocodile of giggling children in blue shorts and white T-shirts were passing on their way to the school playing fields at the end of the road. She no longer needed to wonder if any of them were James or Rebecca. They had both moved on, as well as away, and now she must move on too. But to where?

Registering was an unexpected challenge. First she had to decide on her user-name. It had to be something she could live with but that no one else would recognise as belonging to her. Eventually she decided on Alice, close enough to Alison to feel comfortable but not something she had ever actually been called. It was a good Oxford name too, not to mention that there was something of the confusion of *Through the Looking Glass* in what she was doing anyway. She soon discovered that there were a surprising number of other Alices on the site. She had to be content with Alice29.

Setting up her profile also posed dilemmas. Even deciding on her age took some thought. She tried inputting her true age, fifty. It looked terrible; a concrete accusation of time past, and wasted. Forty-five looked so much better.

Next, a physical description was required. It couldn't be the complete truth as that would leave her vulnerable to being recognised, but not too different or she might forget what she had said. In the end she decided to admit to auburn hair but forget the grey streaks, she would still have hazel eyes but forget the glasses. She made a couple of other small but harmless changes, such as taking off a few kilos when it came to her weight, and adding a few centimetres when it came to her height.

The following section asked about her interests. She unchecked all the options except theatre, reading, travel, and sport; they made her sound intelligent as well as active. There weren't boxes for daytime TV or shopping.

Finally, it asked her what her expectations were from this new relationship. 'What relationship?' she muttered, and immediately clicked *Next*, leaving all the boxes checked.

The screen went blank and stayed blank. Alison straightened up, half relieved that no one was interested in her profile, half irritated that even with the improvements she was still not a cyber-femme fatale.

There was a flicker and the screen was suddenly alive with incoming message alerts. Mr Scarlet, Macho69, and Romeo101, were just a few of the names signalling their need to talk to her. She was aware of an unfamiliar sensation, which took her a few moments to identify. Then she realised; she was a cyber-femme fatale after all. For the first time that day she smiled.

Alison clicked and opened the message from Mr Scarlet. It was not at all what she had expected. Help, she thought, as she read on, can people actually physically do that?

A glance at several of the other messages sent her scurrying back to her profile. On inspection she discovered that the boxes she had left checked indicated that what she expected from the relationship was sex, and in more positions than she had ever previously known existed. She unchecked all the boxes except day trips to Paris, walks in the park and swimming by moonlight. Not that she'd done the latter for more years than she cared to remember.

This time when she clicked *Next*, the screen only went blank for a few seconds and then reappeared saying *Mail*

Box Empty. Alison sighed. There was no one out there who really did just want a bit of romance in their lives. No one at all.

Alison shut the study door firmly behind her and took Chocolate for a walk down Dragon Lane and on towards University Parks. It was a day filled with golden light and the sweet, heady smell of cut grass. She sat on the bank of the Cherwell and watched the punts glide by.

She and Richard had met punting. Actually that wasn't quite true, she had been punting and he had been drowning. Awash with birthday Champagne he had slipped, tumbled out of his punt and disappeared beneath the water. She, and her then boyfriend Pete, had been in the punt behind. Pete, who prided himself on his life-saving skills, had plunged in and dragged Richard half-conscious to the bank. It took just one lop-sided smile and one wink from a sea-green eye and she was lost.

By ten o'clock Alison had had enough of the echoing emptiness of the house and she decided to go to bed. On her way past the study she remembered she had forgotten to switch off the computer. She was just about to log off when she felt the smallest tickle of curiosity. She would check the website, just in case...

One message flashed. She peered at it. *Abelard says Hi.*

Was that Abelard as in *'Abelard and Heloise'*? She remembered reading the play at school. She had been fascinated by the true, but tragic, tale of inappropriate love, misunderstandings and their consequences. Soon after they had met, Richard had taken her to an open air performance on the manicured lawns of Wadham College. They had walked hand in hand between the trees and breathed the sweetness of night-scented honey-suckle. The desire of the lovers in the play had heightened their own desire for each other. She had never expected that this desire could become a blurred memory hidden beyond a veil of nappies, homework and teenage tantrums.

'Hi,' she typed, 'why Abelard?

'To remind me that actions can have consequences!'

'Hopefully not castration and life-long persecution...'

'Not as long as we play by the rules. Why Alice?'

'Maybe because I feel lost just now,' she found herself writing.

'Perhaps I can help. Tell me more about yourself...'

When Alison eventually looked up she was surprised to see the clock on the mantelpiece said it was midnight. As she signed off and climbed the stairs to bed, Alison realised that she knew just enough about Abelard. She knew that he sometimes worked in Oxford, that he was married, that he had children. The precise details of age, sex and number were left deliberately vague; after all she had no need to know. And he knew the same amount about her. She also knew that they could walk past each other in the street and never realise. They had discussed whether they should exchange photos, but somehow the anonymity of not doing so felt so much safer, and more comfortable. Anyway, would he upload a genuine, current photo of himself? And for that matter, would she?

The week that followed was one of the strangest of Alison's life. By day everything went on as normal. She shopped, looked after Chocolate and Atlas, ironed a mountainous backlog of shirts and decided on the colour scheme for the conversion of the children's playroom into a second spare bedroom. However, at eight o'clock she would pour herself a large glass of chilled Chablis and, with an unfamiliar tingle of anticipation, head for the study.

It took just a few clicks and Abelard would be there, and she would immediately be immersed in this new and oddly exciting cyber-world. They discussed books they had read, exhibitions they had seen, plays they had enjoyed. They argued about politics and religion. They agreed on solutions to the problems of global warming and Third World poverty. Alison felt more stimulated and appreciated than she had for years. She and Abelard shared so many interests, sometimes she felt they had travelled through life on the same train, although in separate carriages.

On Thursday, Abelard suggested they meet - just for coffee. Sometime over the weekend perhaps?

'I don't think that's a good idea,' she'd typed frantically, 'we get on so well like this.'

'But we could have so much more and never hurt anyone.'

'I really don't think that's possible, we'll be seen, worse we may not like each other. Our friendship will be ruined.'

'*I know I'll like you. Don't be afraid.*'

'Anyway my husband will be home. I won't be able to get away.'

'*Well, I'm going to stay in Oxford anyway. A friend will put me up. I can't face going home; it's like living in an emotional freezer. So if you change your mind, I'll be around.*'

On Friday morning, Richard rang. 'I'm so sorry, there's one hell of a crisis here. I'm going to have to stay over. I'll be back on Monday.'

An unfamiliar fury gripped Alison. 'For Christ's sake, Richard, apart from anything else the Rutherwoods are coming to supper on Saturday.'

'You'll have to cancel. I'm sure they'll understand. I hope you do too.'

Alison understood all too well. She was going to have a long, dreary, and lonely weekend, while he was living it up in Paris. It was just too much.

Alison spent a long time getting dressed. How did you choose the right clothes to impress at her age? Nothing too formal and certainly nothing frumpy, but nothing that looked like it was 'asking for it' either, so keep it elegant... be in control. Not that Abelard would actually know she was Alice, of course.

Elegant, that's a joke, she thought staring despairingly at her waist. Once it had been slim enough for Richard to put his hands round. If only she had a bit more will power when it came to diets.

Eventually she decided upon a navy T-shirt with a scoop neck and a pair of well-cut white linen trousers. As the sun was blazing down, she slid her sunglasses on so they perched on the top of her head and picked up her new wide-brimmed sun-hat. Wearing that, not even her mother would recognise her.

As she headed for the front door, she also picked up the copy of *Alice in Wonderland* she had promised Abelard she would carry to identify herself – even though it could, and would, stay firmly in her handbag.

Alison arrived half an hour early at The Trout, just outside Wolvercote. She wanted time to find a place to sit where she could observe and yet be unobserved herself. They had agreed on The Trout because it was away from the centre of Oxford and was full of tourists and couples with young families. It would, consequently, be avoided by anyone likely to recognise either of them.

The pub was already busy but she managed to fight her way to the bar. Then, armed with a large glass of Pinot Grigio, she found a small unoccupied table on the terrace. It was half-hidden behind a tree and gave her a discreet view of the several doorways that led inside the pub. She slipped on her sunglasses, pulled her sunhat down so that her face would be lost in its shadow, and sat sipping her wine. She was ridiculously nervous for someone who was not actually going to meet anyone.

The air was full of babbling voices and the roar of the water as it tumbled and foamed over the weir. The sounds blended and blurred into one endless stream. It was strangely soothing and soon Alison felt calmer. Glancing across to the garden on the far side of the river, something grey and still caught her eye. Peering more closely she realised a stone lion was staring unblinkingly at her. A childhood memory stirred. Aslan, of Wardrobe fame. Guardian of the world of Narnia. She could guess what his advice would be regarding the dangerous yet strangely enticing world of internet.

A man smartly dressed in a navy blue blazer sat alone at the table opposite. Maybe he felt her gaze for he glanced at her and smiled - a wonderful smile that lit up his face. Solid build, only a hint of fat, eyes like deep river pools, dark hair with a light dusting of grey at his temples, a tanned, fine-boned face. If only he were Abelard.

But of course he wasn't. Alison watched the condensation mist her glass. She was looking out for a man with no grey hair whatsoever, and who was certainly not even the merest touch overweight – at least that was what his profile had led her to believe. Whether it was more or less accurate than her own profile was still to be discovered. However, she did know that the description could probably refer to a few hundred Oxford men, so to avoid any embarrassing mistakes Abelard would be carrying a copy of *Alice Through the Looking Glass*. Unfortunately this man had no book of any sort.

She waited quietly, sipping her wine, watching the ebb and flow of customers, enjoying the dappling of the sun on the water. She had almost forgotten her mission when someone coughed.

Recognition flared, sending her heart spinning to her stomach. It was impossible - Richard was in Paris. She looked up.

Richard was not in Paris. He was standing in front of the nearest doorway, his eyes sweeping the terrace. She felt sick. How on earth had he found out she was here? She shrank back into the deepest shade, guilt pumping like poison through her body.

It was only then that she realised he hadn't yet seen her. If he would move from the doorway she could slip away. As she waited Alison realised that it wasn't anger that drove his eyes, rather it was expectancy. A moment later he turned abruptly and disappeared back inside the bar. Alison knew that this was her chance to escape but a terrible and overwhelming curiosity held her frozen in her seat. Five minutes later Richard reappeared carrying a pint of lager in one hand, a briefcase in the other. He chose a table at the far side of the terrace and sat down.

The truth exploded within her, and fury replaced guilt. He was waiting for someone. He was the one having an affair, not her. Her fingers tightened on her glass. She would strangle the last breath from his body. Alison was about to stand up and confront him when she realised that then she would have to explain what she was doing there. So she remained where she was.

For a while Richard sat sipping his drink, periodically checking his watch and looking round. After checking his watch for the fifth time, he opened his briefcase and pulled out a book.

It took Alison several seconds to realise the implications of what she was seeing. But as realisation hit her, she had to fight to control the hysteria that churned and bubbled inside her.

God, how stupid she had been not to see it before. Indeed not to realise days ago that that was why she and Abelard had so much in common. Richard was Abelard. He was waiting for her. As for his profile, he had obviously tweaked the truth just as she had.

She took a gulp of wine, letting the cool liquid steady her. So she and Richard were indeed one of the eighty percent of couples who found the idea of adultery attractive. How wonderfully ironic that they had ended up trying to be unfaithful with each other.

Alison choked back the desire to laugh aloud at the ridiculousness of it. She also choked back the desire to rush over and share the joke with Richard. Instinct sparked, warning her to stop and think. The situation was dangerous. If he discovered that she was Alice, then everything would change. The trust that underpinned their marriage would be distorted, maybe destroyed. She was sure she could deal with his attempted infidelity. She was not sure he would be able to deal with hers. Her mother had always told her that there were occasions when things were best left unsaid. This was just such an occasion.

If only she could get out of the pub without being seen, then Richard would eventually give up waiting for Alice to appear and would think up some excuse to come home early. Then it would be up to her to make their marriage work. She knew she could do it, because in spite of all the mundane minutiae and aggravations of the past twenty-five years, she now knew he was still the person he used to be - and that they could fall in love with each other again.

After a few minutes, Richard opened the book and began reading. Alison smiled at the idea of the middle-aged Richard reading a children's book. Taking the opportunity to retreat, she slid out of her seat and slipped into the bar. She made her way through the pub and out into a dazzle of sunlight. She was soon manoeuvring her car out of the car park.

A Mercedes convertible momentarily blocked her way, but all she saw of the driver was a mass of fair hair, cherry-bright lipstick and the flash of a slim bronze hand. Just wait until she's fifty-something, thought Alison with a touch of spiteful irritation. She swung the wheel to the left and headed towards the city centre.

Later that night, as she waited for Richard to call her and explain that his business meeting had been cancelled, she logged on to the website. Abelard was not online. She searched for his user-name and the search came back blank. Abelard was no longer contactable.

Alison smiled and went to let Chocolate out for his evening run. Richard would have learnt his lesson by now. Abelard would be no more, as would Alice. Soon the phone would ring and he would tell her of his earlier than expected return from Paris. She could be warm, sympathetic and get ready to welcome him home.

Midnight passed and the phone didn't ring. Alison made her way reluctantly to bed. But in the morning Richard would call her, she was certain of that. In the end everything had worked out quite perfectly.

Richard had just finished his pint when he was enveloped by a pair of slim, brown arms, and the sweet, muskiness of J'Adore.

'I'm sorry I'm late, darling. The traffic in St Giles was at a standstill.'

The cherry lips smiled at him and Richard pulled her close and kissed them. 'You know that I will forgive you anything.'

The woman sat down, 'So let's have that bottle of Champagne you promised me. Then we're out of here. You've the whole weekend, you said, and we're not going to waste a minute.'

Richard smiled and closed *The Good Hotel Guide* he had been studying, and slipped it back into his brief case. Two whole nights with this wonderful woman, he thought, he was the luckiest man alive. Making his way inside to the bar, he ordered a bottle of Bollinger.

As he carried the bottle and glasses back to the table, a small tremor of guilt flared. He extinguished it at once. Alison would never know; as far as she was concerned he was in Paris and working flat out. Anyway, after twenty-five years of what had become a marriage of habit, surely a fling was only to be expected. And what a fling.

Someone pushed past him, jolting his arm so that Richard nearly dropped the bottle.

'Sorry,' apologised a dark-haired man. He appeared rather flushed to Richard, but then it was rather too hot a day for a blazer.

'You've dropped your book,' said Richard.

'Thanks.' The man picked up the book and, ramming it into his pocket, hurried towards the main door.

Richard watched him for a moment and smiled to himself; it really was quite unusual to see a middle-aged man reading *Alice Through the Looking Glass*. But then they were in Oxford, after all.

AFTER THE PHOENIX

GILLIAN RATHBONE

Directly in front of Rose sat a large woman. With her Sumo shoulders and hair resembling a thatched cottage she obliterated the subtitles of the German film Rose had been so looking forward to. Exasperated, Rose turned round to scan the Phoenix and check whether there were spare seats further back, but the place was packed. It was, after all, a Saturday evening and out of term. It seemed she would have to spend the next couple of hours not knowing what was going on, gathering only an unsatisfactory and probably inaccurate gist. Add to that the irritation of this substantial woman's constant shifting in her seat - as she was now, laughing at all the wrong times, slapping her thighs, leaning slightly forward as if in a come-on to an opponent wrestler. To top it all she was wearing a backpack that thrust her out of line with the other punters and caused more obstruction for Rose.

There was nothing Rose could do. The thought of a blunt instrument caused her some amusement, though even if she'd had one she wouldn't have liked to tackle such a formidable-looking creature. No one else seemed about to say or do anything; it was really only Rose who was affected.

She wondered whether she should go home and come to another showing, but decided against it; she was here now and should try to make the best of it. So she took off her jacket, sat back and tried to relax. Now and then the shoulders in front shifted, usually accompanied by thigh-slapping, and Rose was able to get a glimpse of half a line of subtitle. But this was rather worse than seeing nothing at all. Despite her best efforts she grew increasingly tense and started to develop a headache, so that when the credits finally rolled she could only feel relieved. She watched tight-lipped as the woman stood up. For a moment it seemed to Rose that her body, aided by that large thatched head, obscured the entire screen; she appeared as tall as she was broad.

Of course her hugeness wasn't her fault. On the other hand, it was a good thing that not everyone of her size was so insensitive. If she'd removed that stupid backpack - honestly would you credit it! - and kept still... The woman was shoving her way past others in her row, the one or two who had been attempting to get up and leave submitting like long grass before a lawnmower. She was oblivious to everyone, it appeared, making no eye contact, treading all over people and leaving behind the odd strangled cry - no doubt from those whose feet she had crushed. Dogged and tank-like, she reached the aisle where she proceeded to force her way, like a hard-flung ball scattering skittles, into the cinema foyer.

Rose, meanwhile, got unsteadily to her feet feeling somewhat dazed, and edged along the row of seats. In the foyer, the woman was scrutinising the posters of films forthcoming. Rose was surprised to see that from one of those massive hands dangled the tiniest, daintiest evening bag imaginable. It was made of a black satiny material and the woman held it by its delicate silver chain. Rose was momentarily bewildered by the incongruity, then felt a surge of pity and guilt. It seemed to her as if the woman, coming alone on an evening out, had attempted to give it a sense of occasion by carrying that absurd little bag. Was her behaviour a kind of defiance, an 'all right I know I'm not attractive, nobody will like me but I don't care' act, a putting up of two fingers to the world? Was she lonely?

Rose's thoughts were chaotic. Should she smile at the woman and say something friendly as she passed her to go out into Walton Street? But what would she say, and, if she knew, would she dare say it?

For heaven's sake, she told herself, pull yourself together! Nonetheless she was agitated and remorseful.

She stood irresolute: alright the woman had no idea of what Rose had been feeling, but this didn't get rid of the guilt. She, Rose, had given no time whatever to wondering why a grown woman should behave in such a way, why she had been such a pain and utterly regardless of others.

The woman picked up a Phoenix programme from the box outside and set off along the street, her vast flowered dress tight across the shoulders and flapping round her calves. Rose watched her go, wondering about her destination; where did she live? Would she put the small bag carefully away for the next anti-social event? Rose smiled at her own wit and at once felt bad again.

On an impulse she made up her mind to follow the woman a little way. It was only half past eight and a beautiful evening - much too nice to go straight home. In any case she felt tense. Perhaps she'd find some reassurance, an easing of her pity if she were to discover that the woman at least lived in a nice little house in Jericho or in a flat overlooking Port Meadow. It would be stretching it to hope the woman was going home to someone who loved her, or even to a friend who shared her life. And from the woman's obliviousness, as far as one could tell, to everyone she had encountered that evening, she would surely never cotton on that she was being followed.

Rose grinned sheepishly. What a thing she was contemplating - stalking someone really. But her curiosity as well as her compassion was aroused, and even as these thoughts went through her mind she had set off. In some way, she hoped again, she might be given an opportunity to redeem herself. She played back her earlier ideas of the woman's behaviour - how she might after all be only too aware of others, conscious of how unattractive she was. Oh, Rose thought, exasperated, here we go again. I'm not analysing, I'm ruminating as always, going round and round like a hamster on a wheel and getting nowhere.

The woman moved swiftly, hogging the pavement, the swaying motion brought about by her ungainliness taking her from one side to the other and forcing anyone approaching to step into the gutter. Rose followed; maybe there was no one waiting at home for the woman but there could be a dog or a cat or something. She giggled a bit hysterically, unhappy with what she was doing, and suddenly confronted herself: how much of all this was because she couldn't face going back to her own empty flat, especially in the middle of a weekend when it seemed the world was made up of couples - except for the woman, of course. If only she and Chas...

Well, it was her doing, she'd known he would accept the post, it would have been madness to throw away the chance. And he wanted her to go with him, he said he loved her and she certainly loved him. But was that enough? The thought of leaving Oxford let alone England... Oh life could be so bloody painful. And look at her now, spending the evening stalking! She had to smile at herself. And anyway, perhaps she had it all wrong. Perhaps the woman was just a fat slob. But, that tiny bag...

Rose was near to tears. The woman barged on past Oxford University Press and Worcester College, turning the corner at the traffic lights. It looked as if she were headed for the railway station. Rose hesitated - well, what should she do now, turn back? But it was still too early to go home. She came to a sudden decision and at once felt a burden lift: I'll ring Chas when we - I - get to the station. She felt in her bag: yes, she'd got her mobile. I'll see if he wants to meet up for a glass of wine or something. She hadn't seen him since, well... he had in fact rung her and suggested talking things over this evening. But Rose hadn't been able to face it. Anyway, she'd told herself, she really wanted to see that German film. She'd known it wouldn't be Chas's cup of tea.

The woman was definitely making for the station; she lumbered on, planting down now one trunk leg then shifting her awesome bulk on to the other, each arm held slightly away from her body and one fat finger curled around the slender chain of the evening bag. Rose was able to keep up her normal pace behind her and even, now and then, to forget her in the anticipation - and sudden excitement at the thought - of seeing Chas.

Crab-like, the woman scaled the station steps, Rose following, and waded inside. She cut through a gaggle of tourists and made straight for the Ladies' lavatories. Rose found an empty table in the refreshment area and sat down.

A few minutes passed and a couple of girls emerged from the Ladies. All at once Rose was struck by the enormity of her actions - sitting there in the station, keeping an eye on the Ladies for all the world like some seedy private eye. She didn't know whether to laugh or cry. Imagine making a mystery out of a rude woman's decision to carry a minute evening bag! Wasn't this Oxford after all - full of weirdos?

In that moment the remainder of her curiosity and pity dissipated. She felt her cheeks burn and began scrambling into her jacket, pushing an arm into the wrong sleeve till she gave up the attempt altogether. She was on her feet when the door to the Ladies was pushed open again. A small elderly lady came out dragging a case on wheels, and, hard behind her, a powerful-looking figure in jeans and t-shirt, backpacked, a face wreathed in scowls, and quite, quite bald.

TWO TIMERS

LAURA KING

1887

M adeleine Mountfield stirred and gazed at the walnut Napoleon mantle clock, courtesy of a narrow shaft of light through the velvet drapes. Nearly four o'clock. She'd been asleep for most of the day. In the next room she heard her newborn begin to cry. She reached out and rang the bell for the wet nurse. Presently the crying subsided.

How pleased she had been to present Charles with a son for his firstborn. He had so wished for it. It had been a lengthy and arduous labour and at one point Dr Frewin had thought she would not survive it and the Vicar had better be summoned. With moments between herself and a certain grave, the fever had finally broken. She was dimly aware of a certain clammy squeezing of her hand, a fleeting expression in the gaslight as relief was sighed all round and, far away, a baby crying.

Now here she was a week later, still weak and liable to die at the slightest provocation.

She and Charles had yet to settle on a name, having not wished to tempt fate before the infant's arrival. She only hoped she'd still be awake by the time Charles came home, as he seldom returned from the Works before ten at night and Madeleine presently struggled to keep her eyes open after eight. She looked at the impressive arrangement of flowers from Charles on the dresser - yellow roses, her favourite, and the smaller bouquet beside it of seasonal flowers from his office scout Sarah; however had she afforded it? Perhaps she had picked them from the borders of Christ Church Meadow and arranged them herself.

She imagined her husband Charles at the Printworks; Theology papers today, according to his note. She hoped she'd soon feel well enough to take a turn around the park with him on a Sunday as they had been wont to do before their new addition.

Two weeks later, Madeleine managed both Church and luncheon with Charles. He could not have been more attentive and appeared delighted when Madeleine said she felt strong enough for an afternoon stroll with Nanny pushing the perambulator containing young Halstead Vickery, as Charles had named him. Nanny walked a few yards ahead with Madeleine on Charles' arm and Charles himself tapping his silver-topped cane with his initials engraved on it; a wedding present from his wife, which he felt, befitted his status. Various neighbours and acquaintances stopped to pay their respects. At least one dinner invitation ensued, but was politely declined by Charles. When they returned home to Mansfield Road, Madeleine was greatly fatigued but insisted on joining Charles in the drawing room.

'You're very pale, my dear,' he said, placing his cane carefully in the hall stand and brushing her face with his hand. 'You've over-exerted yourself. Allow me to help you upstairs.'

'In a moment, Charles,' she said, reclining on the chaise longue. 'I cannot tell you how good it is to be out and in society again. But is there a reason we must turn down every invitation?'

'You need time to recover, Madeleine.'

'Not too long I trust.'

'God willing.' Charles opened his cigar case and lit one.

'Do you think we might have days such as this more often Charles? You work such long hours; I scarcely see you and it surely cannot be recommended for your own health to enjoy so little leisure.'

'Perhaps at the end of the finals, dearest. It is our busiest time of year, as you know. And you have been so terribly ill; Dr Frewin recommended that you should not be taxed in any way.'

'That is considerate of him,' said Madeleine, 'but I believe I can manage a conversation with my husband a little more often than once every three weeks.'

'You don't object to the name...?'

'No, Charles. Halstead Vickery is most fitting. It was just a little surprising to find out after it was chosen, rather than before.'

'Madeleine, do let me help you to your room. You look as though you might faint.'

Madeleine allowed him to take her upstairs, where her maid undressed her and put her to bed.

Weeks passed and Madeleine slowly regained her strength and recommenced her rounds of visiting and charitable works in the mornings followed by walks with Nanny and Halstead in the afternoons. Sundays, when Charles could manage both Church and luncheon, continued to be rare, except for Halstead's christening, although he did regularly bid her goodnight when he arrived home each night.

One afternoon, just as Madeleine and Nanny were preparing to leave for a walk in University Parks, the doorbell rang. The door was opened and, without waiting to be announced, Mr Robert Landrey stepped inside.

'My dear lady!' he exclaimed removing his hat and kissing her on the cheek. 'I thought it high time I dropped in on you to offer my hearty congratulations; not a bad time I trust. My, he's a bonny little fellow. Your cheekbones, if I'm not very much mistaken, and your eyes, Mrs Mountfield. Or, may I address you by your prettier name?'

'Oh, I'd rather you didn't, Mr Landrey.'

'Never mind, Mrs Mountfield. I'm merely pleased to see you with some colour back in your cheeks. Let me present you with a trifle for young Halstead V.'

And with that, Charles's business partner produced a small brown package from his inside coat pocket. Mrs Mountfield unwrapped it to find a wooden teether.

'Of course, he may be a little young...'

'That's quite alright Mr Landrey. I shall keep it for him.'

'I see you're about to go for a stroll. Don't mind if I join you I hope? Have you seen all the splendid new villas being erected on Banbury Road? It won't be the same now the Dons are all marrying. Some say it will be the end of Oxford University as we know it.'

'Please do join us, Mr Landrey.' Madeleine responded with a frozen smile.

'Robert, please.'

Robert Landrey continued to make polite conversation, mostly one-sided. Once at the park gates though, when Nanny was some yards ahead pushing the perambulator, he caught Madeleine's arm and turned her to face him. 'Madeleine, please forgive me but I must speak to you in confidence. I am concerned.'

'Concerned?' she repeated, her eyes widening.

'Yes. Concerned for your welfare. Concerned you are not being taken care of - properly.'

'What do you mean, Mr Landrey? Charles is a good man.'

'Are you certain? Where do you suppose he is every night until ten o'clock, six nights a week? At the Works? When I myself seldom finish beyond seven. Moreover, how do you suppose his office scout affords her own unshared lodgings in Jericho?'

'Mr Landrey, I will not listen to this offensive slander! How dare you say such things to me! One more word of this nature and I shall never speak to you again!'

Robert Landrey winced, but held his ground.

'Madeleine, I know this must come as a terrible shock, but I firmly believe you are a neglected wife.'

Madeleine turned away and observed Nanny watching her with a worried frown.

'Do what you will with this knowledge, Madeleine. Just remember that I am at your disposal if ever you should need a protector or comforter.'

Madeleine's eyes blazed as she signalled to Nanny that she would catch her up. 'And what of your wife Mr Landrey?'

'I have no wife, Madeleine, only arrangements. 'I knew from youth that I was not a marrying man. It grieves me to see the damage my fellow men inflict who should know better.'

For the rest of the day Madeleine held herself together while inside a cyclone of emotions whirled. She determined she would confront Charles that night. But it was almost a week, and only after he had commented on her pallor and even suggested a visit from Dr Frewin, before she found the courage to speak.

'Charles, you should know that your business partner visited me last week.'

'Ah yes,' he said, stroking the top of his cane as was his habit. 'He said he had something to give young HV - and before the boy started University. He *is* a wag.'

'He was most ill-mannered.'

'A little rough around the edges, I'll grant you, but he is from Rotherhithe. However, he and his money did join the Works at a crucial time. Without him, I don't know what would have become of...'

'Charles,' Madeleine interrupted, but hesitated before asking, 'why are you so late returning home each night?'

Charles fiddled with his cigar. 'I told you dearest, we possess an order book as long as your arm to clear by this Friday, Anatomy this week, Algebra the next, Modern Classicism the following. In other words, to keep you in silk dresses and our son in the finest swaddling clothes, not to mention the best nannies, dear Madeleine. But then I don't expect you to understand the ways of the world.'

'Damn it, Charles, I found you that girl from the orphanage to help in the office when times were hard, not for any other reason. Not so that you could set her up in her own Jericho lodgings while I wait for you every night alone, with only the servants for company. Has the girl no shame? Have you no shame? No, I don't suppose she could refuse could she, in her position.'

'Damn and blast the man - what poisonous nonsense has he been filling your head with? I never expected to hear such vitriol from your lips. I suppose he also suggested himself as your comforter?'

Madeleine remained silent.

'Just as I suspected. And did you succumb? Did you?'

'Really Charles, how could you! You presume I would take Mr Landrey's word over my own husband's?'

'He's had his eye on you for a long time. I've even heard it said in the Turl Street tavern that he chose to invest his capital in the Works on the strength of his attachment to you.'

'If I wanted words, those were not the ones I wanted from you Charles. It's too late for words. Last night, knowing sleep would not come yet again, I decided to settle the matter once and for all. I donned my parlour maid's hood and cloak and waited for you at the Printworks. When you emerged, just after seven, I followed you at a distance, all the way to Juxon Street. I saw her admit you.'

'You did what? My own wife spying on me like a common guttersnipe!'

'I had to know, Charles. I had to know if Mr Landrey spoke the truth, for my own sanity's sake. Don't you see?'

Charles was silent for a moment. 'I think I do Madeleine.'

'I must insist that she leaves, Charles, at once. I don't care what becomes of her but she must leave Oxford and never return.'

'My dear Madeleine. I can solemnly promise you that you need never suffer a sleepless night on my account again. You will never see Sarah again.'

The last thing Madeleine saw was a cushion coming towards her face. The last sensation she felt was a gold tassel against her neck.

2007

Marilyn Menvier stirred and hazily eyed the walnut Napoleon mantle clock courtesy of a chink in the wood-effect blinds. Nearly four o'clock; she'd been asleep for most of the day. In the next room she heard her newborn start to cry. She reached out and rang for the au pair to bring him to her. How pleased she was that they had been blessed with little Harvey Vaughn as their firstborn. Not least after the drama of his birth, following an endless labour and midwife shortages, only to appear after the surgical team had prepped her for a C-section, though not before necessitating two blood transfusions. She was told afterwards that she had nearly died and her husband Clark had been advised to summon the hospital chaplain, just in case.

And now five months of maternity leave loomed, both too long and too short. She imagined Clark presiding over the meeting to thrash out the final details of the takeover of Meadowprint by Inkings of Oxford. How fine he had looked in his new suit this morning, the blue-grey setting off his matching eyes, and how powerful in an age where hardly any man bothered to wear one. She would have gone weak at the knees except she was still punch drunk from having Harvey and her tender state was not about to ping back into 'sex kitten' any time soon. A small price to pay, she thought looking down at her baby, but I'm still damned if I'm going to be the only one, health or not! 'Anyway, you're all Daddy's fault, aren't you, little man?' she teased aloud.

She scooped Harvey from his cot and a kind of contentment descended as she rocked back and forth in her nursing mother's glider chair, a present from her parents.

On the dresser less practical presents in the form of a large bouquet of freesias from Clark and a hardly less extravagant spray from Samantha, his PA, wafted their scent toward her. The dear girl, however had she afforded it when she was trying to save up a deposit for that flat share she was planning with her old school friend? Marilyn didn't make it to the Inkings office very often, because of her own full-time job as an Oxfam fundraiser, but she tried to show an interest and keep up with the burgeoning world of print-on-demand. And more than once when times were leaner she'd mucked in during the summer when she and Clark should have been taking a holiday. Now it was big and mean enough to swallow another company and they could afford Harvey and private education at last. She sighed. If only Clark didn't have to work such long hours, everything would be perfect.

As the weeks passed, Marilyn was   absorbed into a round of mother and baby coffee mornings and working a little from home while Astrid, the au pair, watched Harvey. Cutteslowe and University Parks were the objects of regular jaunts from the Portland Road house, although sometimes Marilyn simply liked to stroll along the streets of Summertown or into Oxford pushing Harvey in his V2 Explorer buggy, giving Astrid the afternoon off. She particularly enjoyed the antiques market at Gloucester Green every Thursday and Mallams auction rooms where she'd often pick up odds and ends, Victorian mostly, though she kept telling herself she really ought to focus on art deco and bakelite items for a 1930's house. Clark was more of a modernist, which made their home a real mish-mash, although at least he'd liked the Napoleon mantle clock. It was in the auction rooms that she'd found the silver-topped cane with the initials CM engraved on the top. Such a coincidence, she thought, could not be ignored – she had to have it.

She couldn't wait to show it to Clark, and after checking Harvey was still comfortably asleep in his buggy, she sped off down to the Inkings of Oxford offices in the former Cooper's marmalade factory off Hollybush Walk. The offices were deserted except for Jeffrey the graphic designer who was working on a book jacket for a client.

'Hocus Focus?' she enquired, looking over his shoulder.

He glanced up and smiled at her. 'A psychic investigator – surprisingly, not entirely round the loop. Not like some of them who don't even have the excuse of a wacky subject.'

'Have you read it then?'

'Nah, just skimmed it to get a feel for the cover. All you have time for when you're knocking five a week out, although I did hang on to the Motorcross one for a couple of weeks and read every page.' He winked. 'My favourite job this year. And we've had a good run on them too which is always ace.'

'When's Clark back again?'

Jeffrey shifted uncomfortably. 'I think he and Sam will be gone most of the afternoon.'

'Another Meadowprint meeting?'

'Um. I think so.'

'I don't know why he has to take her with him - I'd have thought a PA's place is in the office. Pretty unfair to expect you to man the phones on top of your own work.'

'No comment.'

'Jeffrey, is there something I should know?'

'Search me,' he replied, rising from his chair. 'But if it's more than just a meeting...' He began removing his glasses and met her eyes. 'You know I've always found you very attractive, Marilyn.'

He grasped her forearm and seemed about to lock her in a passionate embrace. Marilyn broke away and grabbing the buggy, fled from the building in tears.

She ran all the way home to Summertown, uncaring that the heavens opened just past St Giles' church or that Harvey awoke and decided to cry his head off as they sped past Park Town. This set her off again and it was all she could do to calm herself every time she had to pass someone. Could it really be true?

A week went by as Marilyn put off the inevitable confrontation and grew more and more depressed.

Then one evening when Marilyn was alone yet again, Harvey in bed, and Astrid experimenting with a new hair colourant in the bathroom, the telephone rang. It was

Sonia from work to ask how she was. Before Marilyn knew it she was confessing how miserable and alone she felt, though without mentioning her suspicions.

'Sounds like the baby blues to me!' Sonia said cheerfully. 'Suffered them myself with the second one. I know how you feel. What they don't tell you is once they leave to go to College, you get 'em all over again!'

Marilyn smiled despite herself.

'No, what you need is a damned good night out my girl. Shake the cobwebs off. Show Clark you're not just a little wait-at-home wifie. Listen, would that au pair of yours be able to babysit tomorrow night? A few of us are going to a psychic evening in Didcot for a laugh. Would you be up for that?'

'Hmm, I don't know. I've never been. What do they do?'

'Oh lots of things, palm reading, object reading, tea leaf reading probably. But it's all a load of crystal balls! Just want to know if I should change my lottery numbers really - been using the same bleeders for five years and haven't won a bean! Come on, it'll be a laugh. Jackie from Accounts got a message from her auntie that she'd meet a dark handsome stranger last time. And she did. A stunning black cat with amber eyes appeared at the door the very next day eating the bird food and she's been stuck with Archie ever since.'

'I'm not sure.'

'Well ready or not, we're picking you up at six-thirty, so just be dressed and organise that sprogcare ok?'

'I suppose.'

'Well we can arrange to get your teeth pulled if you'd rather, but we reckon this might be more fun. See ya!' And with that the line went dead.

The following evening saw Marilyn at the psychic fair in Didcot Civic Hall, clutching the silver-topped cane which she'd felt compelled to bring as her object, a last minute impulse, though she couldn't think why. She looked at all the various tables dotted around and wondered which queue to join. Sonia and her two friends plumped for Gypsy Rose Lee with the largest gold hoop earrings, most metallic turban and most vulgar collection of crystal talisman around her neck, who also happened to have the longest queue. Marilyn ignored their entreaties to join them and set off to find the dullest-looking psychic in the room. She finally spied an elderly lady in tweeds with no queue who claimed, according to her board, to read objects.

Marilyn gave her the cane. The psychic gestured to her to sit down and closed her eyes in concentration.

'I see a lady and a baby. The lady is sad. Her husband works long hours and seldom comes home. She has heard he might have another. She is looking out of a window.'

'What else?' Marilyn asked impatiently, 'What else do you see?'

'She lives in a nice house in the city of Oxford. I see the letter M. I see it twice.'

Marilyn turned pale.

'May I ask; do you dress up my dear?'

'Dress up? How?' asked Marilyn.

'In long dresses. Like the Victorians.'

'No of course not. Well not since a College Ball a long time ago.'

'That's not it my dear. This is a very old cane. It has a history. It witnessed something.'

'What?'

'I see the lady called M confronting her husband. He has a cushion in his hands. She is not moving any more. He shouts for the servants. My dear, something bad happened, something very bad and there is a possibility it could happen again.'

'But it's only a cane I picked up in an auction!'

'But why did you pick it up? Because you recognized it, my dear. And does it not have an astonishing co-incidence attached to it?'

At this Marilyn fled the hall, leaving her friends behind with no explanation. She ran into town desperately searching for a taxi, her mind in turmoil. Eventually she found one and convinced its recalcitrant driver she needed to get back to Oxford. Only one thought dominated her mind. She must take Harvey and leave Clark immediately.

An accident had caused the ring road to close, forcing the taxi to divert through town. As it took the right hand fork onto Banbury Road Marilyn was momentarily transported back to when the old houses were being built on the fields bordering University Parks. She closed her eyes tightly and when she opened them again she saw Summertown - in 2007.

However her relief was short-lived, when turning at last into Portland Road, she saw Clark's Alfa Romeo in the driveway. Luckily he was busy in his study and did not hear her enter and creep up the stairs to pack her things. She packed some essentials into an overnight case. Then she went into Harvey's room and packed a bag for him. Just as she was about to scoop him up, she heard Clark coming up the stairs.

'Marilyn?' he enquired, popping his head round the door. 'You didn't mention you were going out tonight.'

'Oh, just some work mates. They insisted it was time I had a night out.'

'Good idea. Where did you go?'

'Didcot Civic Hall,' she replied, trying to kick the overnight bag out of sight behind the cot.

'Ah that famous Mecca of happening nightlife.' He teased. Then his expression changed as he noticed her movements. 'Marilyn, what's going on? You leaving me for someone else?'

'No.' she replied truthfully.

'Then what? What's with the overnight bag? What were you going to do with Harvey?'

'I just need to get away for a while.'

'What? Without discussing it with me?'

'Yes! You're hardly ever here anyway. What do you care?' Marilyn blurted out.

'I care a great deal. I am your husband after all.'

'I just need to go to my parents for a few days Clark. Get my head straight. I just want to feel, you know, safe.'

'Marilyn, you *are* safe,' said Clark gently, 'or perhaps I should call you by the name you were christened in our previous life – Charles. It was to be my turn to kill you in this lifetime to equalise the karma between us, but frankly I haven't the heart. I decided to leave it at teaching you a lesson by having an affair with my secretary. Oh, and putting you through the horrendous childbirth experience that I suffered.'

'Madeleine?' enquired the voice weak with shock, as a stream of disturbingly vivid images – or were they memories - came flooding into her mind, thick and fast.

Five minutes later found Marilyn lying on the bed propped up with pillows, Clark holding a glass of water to her lips.

'Yes Charles,' continued Clark. 'I know it'll come as the most tremendous shock but we've switched genders. I was Madeleine. You were Charles. Well you *were* the most frightful chauvinist last time round. I wasn't putting up with that again. But basically I love you and forgive you for that, and for killing me last time round. Divorce really would have been the ruin of you in those days and you were only just getting the Printworks back into the black.'

'So that was *my* cane all along?' Marilyn murmured weakly.

'Yes CM was Charles Mountfield and you remembered enough to recognise it, bless you! And our Napoleon clock! But you're Marilyn now.'

'A murderer?' cried Marilyn.

'As was I in our lifetime together in 18th Century Rotterdam as a desperate, failing silk merchant whose demanding wife was a burden too far. But one of us had to break the cycle Marilyn.'

'H... how did you know? When?'

'Well, according to my mother I began to jabber about a previous existence when I was four, but naturally she dismissed it as something I must have seen on television. Then as an adolescent I experienced a series of disturbing visions which led me to find our grave in St Cross churchyard one Saturday. And the house two streets away where we used to live in Mansfield Road. Other memories quickly followed and clicked into place. Everything. Including my time in the inter-realm where we make our choices for each lifetime. The victim always gets to choose, Marilyn. That's how it works. We can repeat the pattern if we want vengeance, or we can choose to break it if we aspire to higher things. Finally I met you as a fresher at the Wonderland ball at St Catz in that stunning Victorian gown and I knew it wasn't just my imagination. You and I really were destined to be together.'

'Were you ever going to tell me?'

'I wanted to, many times, especially when things started going pear-shaped between us again after Harvey was born. But you've got to admit, it's pretty hard to find the right moment, Marilyn. I mean it's not the sort of bombshell you can drop into an everyday conversation without being dragged off by the men in white coats. Ultimately I had to trust that woman's intuition of yours to kick in when the time was right and offer me a helping hand.

'I realise it's an awful lot to take in, but you will get used to it all, in time. I did. On the plus side, I do recall persuading them to make you as pretty as I was! Anyway, leave Harvey, or should I say, Halstead Vickery, to his slumbers and come and have a brandy. We need to talk. It's been a long time.'

THE THIEF OF MAGDALEN BRIDGE

MARY CAVANAGH

Rosalind Lawrence was born in Chipping Campden, a small town near the Oxfordshire/Gloucestershire border, in 1925. She was the youngest child of three, and the only girl. By the age of seventeen she was renowned as the town's beauty. Her skin was like porcelain, her eyes were a cool luminous green, her hair a silky halo of light auburn, and her body a perfect hourglass. When she walked down the street men would smile widely, gasp at her loveliness, and dream dreams of holding her in their arms. Women would smile in friendship, but in truth be tight-lipped with jealousy.

Her father, the headmaster of the town's grammar school, was overly protective of her, and any humble suitors were firmly notified they had no chance of winning his Princess.

Harold Lawrence knew that one day a man of considerable means would ask for her hand and Rosalind would be elevated to a Queen. She would live in a fine house with servants and large grounds, and want for nothing. Naturally, with her future assured, his daughter had no need to work, and thus she spent her days in the company of her mother, learning the art of the perfect wife and visiting the poor and needy.

As part of her twenty-first birthday celebrations Rosalind's father announced that the whole family would be taking a day trip to the city of Oxford. They would go to a jewellers of quality to buy a very special birthday gift, lunch at The Mitre, take a gentle tour around the colleges, and take afternoon tea in The Randolph Hotel. After the constraints of wartime, and only knowing the boundaries of a small sleepy town in the Cotswolds, this was indeed the high life for all of them.

On the morning of the trip the Lawrence family set off very early in the Morris Ten to drive the thirty-six miles at a steady pace. On arrival the car was parked in King Edward Street, and when Harold Lawrence got out of the car he stood on the pavement, holding his hat to his chest, drinking in his memories. 'There it is,' he exclaimed, pointing his finger at the breathtaking beauty of Oriel College, resplendent in early autumn sunshine. 'My *alma mater*; 1908 to 1911.' The family walked across the cobbles to the entrance and moved inside to admire the sun-kissed mullions and green-grassed quadrangles, linking and twisting with a mediaeval magic. They were proud they were not just dull unknowing tourists but an esteemed family with University connections. The fact made them all stand tall, adopt condescending expressions, and sashay off to find Rowell and Harris, the finest jewellers in the High Street.

Rosalind and her parents sat on small gilt chairs whilst a pair of earnest assistants bought trays of brooches, necklaces and rings for them to consider. Her parents clearly favoured a string of genuine oyster pearls for which Rowell and Harris were famed, but the choice was allowed to be her own. After much indecision, trying on, and examining herself in a hand mirror, she chose an antique Victorian piece; an exquisite brooch of around three inches in diameter, set in gold and encrusted with diamonds, emeralds and seed pearls. 'Such excellent taste,' the morning coated manager concurred. 'So fitting with madam's colouring. It can also be worn as a pendant on a chain for evening wear, and may I be so bold to say as a centre piece to a bride's veil.' Rosalind blushed. Her parents nodded approvingly.

When they came out of the jewellery shop Rosalind begged that she be allowed to wear it. 'Oh please Pa,' she said. 'Let me wear it. Just for a little while. It'll be quite safe. There's a good security chain and pin.'

'Oh very well,' Harold Lawrence conceded. 'Just this once, mind you. After that it's for high days and holidays only.'

His wife squeezed his arm and whispered under her breath. 'And certainly for a bride's veil, Harry. She's going to look a picture.'

'She certainly is, Mother. She certainly is,' agreed her husband.

With a great display of ceremony he pinned the brooch on Rosalind's lapel. 'There,' he said. 'That *does* look a treat. Happy birthday to my Princess.'

The family moved slowly, with even more haughtiness and elevation, down the High Street, admiring and commenting on the ancient architecture of church and college, until they reached Magdalen Bridge. 'Will you take my photograph on the bridge, Pa?' asked Rosalind. 'It's such a beautiful setting.' Rosalind took up a position in the middle of the bridge, and turned and laughed as her father clicked the button on the standard Box Brownie. 'Make sure you get a close-up of my lovely brooch,' she called.

One, two, three, four, five shots were taken of the happy young birthday girl. 'Smile, darling, smile. That's lovely. You look every inch the film star today.'

After the shots were completed Rosalind's parents stood discussing how much was left on the spool, and fussily putting the camera away in its case. Her brothers, becoming a little bored, wasted time looking over the bridge's balustrades into the Cherwell River below. When they all turned back a tramp was standing close to Rosalind. Far, far too close, and he seemed to be talking to her. Her mother screamed. Her father shouted, 'Stop Thief.' Her brothers rushed over, grabbed the man, punched him hard in the face, and brought their knees up to his groin. When he fell to the floor they kicked his head and called him names. A small stunned group of passers-by had gathered. 'Our sister is wearing a valuable diamond brooch,' the brothers explained. 'He was trying to steal it.' The passers-by tutted, and nodded, but not wanting to be further involved in the fracas continued on to wherever they were going. As the man lay in agony on the ground the Lawrence family, shaking with shock, moved smartly off the bridge, marching Rosalind as if she was under arrest.

The story of the assault, and their part in thwarting it, was circulated around Chipping Campden with great embellishment by the brothers. One of them was a cub reporter on the local newspaper and the story made the headlines, *'Local men forced to defend their sister from a jewel thief in Oxford. Vagrant attempts robbery in broad daylight.'* Any suitors in the town who still desired the hand of Rosalind Lawrence were now even more discouraged. Who could possibly penetrate two such powerful bodyguards?

Over time her brothers married and moved away. Her spirit dimmed. Her mother fell ill and died, and Rosalind was doomed to the role of unpaid housekeeper to her father. The years passed slowly and she met no one new. Her hair turned grey, her shoulders drooped, and she became old before her time. When her father died in the late nineteen-seventies it was far too late for her to build a new life.

Now Rosalind is a frail elderly lady and her beauty has disappeared, not only to her face but in the folklore of the town. But she remembers. She has a photograph of herself as a smiling young woman, taken on Magdalen Bridge in Oxford in 1946. There has not been a day in her life that she doesn't think about the young man who spoke to her on the bridge that day. The lovely man with the soft cultured voice, the gentle manners, the kind smile, and the pale blue eyes.

At twenty-eight years old, Gerald had been a first year law student at Christ Church College. An ex-air force officer, and part of *'The Few'*, he had at last been free to pursue his academic studies. It had been a fine, warm September morning and, dressed in an old, worn track suit, he'd been for a run along the River Cherwell in training for the University's rugby trials. His clothes had become wet and spattered with mud, and his face ran with sweat. As he crossed over Magdalen Bridge, on his way back to college, he stopped to get his breath, and noticed a smart middle-aged man taking a photograph of a young woman. A girl, really. She was the most beautiful girl he'd ever seen. When the photography was completed he walked up to her, stopped and smiled, and spoke to her. 'It's a beautiful day isn't it?'

'Yes,' she smiled back. 'Oxford is such a magical place.'

'You look very happy.'

'I am. It's my birthday. My twenty-first. My father has just bought me this lovely brooch.'

Gerald was just about to reach for his wallet to retrieve one of his visiting cards. He would suggest that she and her family might like to come to Christ Church to take afternoon tea with him, but suddenly he was grabbed, called a thief, and kicked, and punched to the floor. No one stopped to help him to his feet or find out if he was injured. By the time he managed to stand up the lovely girl had disappeared.

Gerald is now over ninety years old but he forces himself to take a daily walk. He hauls himself to his feet and whistles for Digger, his Dachshund. Walking is the perfect time for remembering. He can still recall her cloud of silky auburn hair, her green eyes and the gentle curve of her cheekbones. Her smile, her perfect pearly teeth, her slender creamy neck and the sweet sound of her voice. He married in his thirties and had three fine sons. He supposes that he has had a reasonable life, but there was always something missing. There has not been a single day in over sixty years that Lord Gerald Fitzgerald hasn't thought about the beautiful girl on the bridge.

SPACE FOR DREAMS

RAY PEIRSON

'Star Light, Star Bright,' Tara said.

She leaned over the safety rail and rubbed a clear patch in the dusty patina on the yellowing plastic of the window. She coughed as some loose dust particles from the old books nobody read any more caught her throat. She avoided looking directly at the dim reflection of her face. Even so, she raised more dust as she touched her hair back into shape by the hand not smeared by the grime on the window.

John was attempting to see past her through the clear patch and clicked his tongue as she managed to block the view. Tara and John always met in this library compartment, known for some long forgotten reason as the Bodleian, because it was deserted and faced in the right direction. She ducked down so she was lined up with the little patch. John lined up with her, cheek to cheek.

'There! You can just see it. Next to that very bright star cluster.'

John rolled his eyes up to the ceiling. 'That star cluster is the Lesser Magellenic Cloud,' he replied in his navigator-student superior voice. 'It's nearly a Galaxy in its own right.'

'Whatever,' she dismissed. 'There! Can you see it? Every time I come down here to look for it, I have to search carefully. It keeps on moving.'

'Surely, to be precise, it is us who are moving?' He was still using his superior voice but he didn't press the point. He was looking where she was pointing with unfeigned interest. 'We're down to a tenth of a light year, give or take. That was the last time I asked and that was weeks ago.'

They looked at the point of light, now almost a disc, for a while.

'You've got to admit it's pretty exciting. I'm sixteen years old and this is the first star that I've been close enough to actually see it move. Mummy remembers Delta Proxima 4 close up but that was over thirty years ago on the last fly-by. It always gets to me. The stars are so far away that however fast we move they just stay still. Sort of indifferent.'

She frowned, and considered. 'Why do the old books and poems from Earth talk about stars twinkling? Did they twinkle in the actual Oxford on Earth? What's wrong with them here? It's not fair. Twinkling sounds nice. Sort of romantic? Eyes twinkle, so why have stars stopped twinkling?'

John did his eyes to the ceiling bit again but his heart wasn't in it. He had once had the same puzzlement until his father had reminded him that the Earth had a thick atmosphere. He explained.

'Oh,' she said without great interest, 'but please stop being so superior.'

'Why? After all, I am superior!' She ignored this old cross-gender joke.

He couldn't leave it be. 'You haven't paid attention to anything outside the ship, have you?'

'Why bother? It only matters if we actually get somewhere. And we have! At last! Isn't it great!'

John failed to make the right noises and she looked into his face. 'We have got somewhere, haven't we? You haven't heard of any snags?'

There was too long a pause. She watched the various expressions cross his face as he decided on his reply.

'No,' he said at last but the bald statement was spoken with a sufficient lack of sincerity for her to reach for his sleeve to gain attention.

'Surely they have clocked three planets already? Three rock-type planets, not gas giants. The right distance from the star in the Cinderella zone – not too hot and not too cold. Any of them could be like Earth.'

'So?' He avoided her gaze.

'This is our fifth fly-by, and we've never been so lucky before. Our first three had no planets to speak of, not a single damn planet. And the next one, GC5467. And Delta Proxima! Those methane atmospheres. Those stinking methane planets. Nothing small enough. Nothing warm enough. Nothing nice enough to build a new City of Oxford like we are supposed to.'

'No, nothing nice enough,' replied John, 'Very unlucky. But we mustn't be too optimistic. We could be unlucky yet again. We have to plan for bad news.'

Tara grasped his sleeve more firmly. 'This time we'll be lucky, I feel it. I feel it here!' She slapped her chest where she assumed her heart was beating. 'We have three chances of a liveable planet. There may be more we haven't spotted yet. This looks to me like a very friendly star. Sun, I mean. It will be a lucky Sun. It will be our Sun. Just like the people on Earth, back in Oxford, had their own Sun.'

She reached for John's hand and crossed two of his fingers for luck. They stood for a long time in silence in the empty compartment. Their hands stayed together.

Eventually Tara blinked and returned from wherever she had been, and said, 'If I hadn't seen the old videos of Earth I couldn't possibly believe in planets. Won't it be funny tottering about on the outside of a large ginormous lump of rock? I'll fall off, I'm sure I will. And there'll be wild animals. Lions! Tigers! And wind. Hurricanes! And rain. I shall have an umbrella. I've always wanted an umbrella. A large red one like in that old movie. It'll be very scary.' She clutched his hand more tightly for protection but smiled as well.

'John?'

'Mm?'

'Just in case... well, if we were unlucky here, where do we go next?'

John hesitated. 'Father tells me things that are supposed to be secret. There was a plan but nobody expected us to take so long to find somewhere. In Oxford, long ago on Earth, when they sponsored our colonisation trip, they were too optimistic. Nobody expected it to take so long. They thought we would find oodles of real estate, nice earth-like planets, just begging for us to move in…'

'If only…' she said with feeling.

'Yes! If only! We've tried the most likely star systems already. The next best is Beta Maxima 464. It's the closest star left on the list of 'possibles' that they hoped we would never need.' He closed his mouth firmly.

'You mean we'll be sifting through the dregs?'

John didn't reply.

She looked searchingly into his eyes, and finally asked her question. 'How close is close?'

'I'm not supposed to know.'

'But your father is Chief Navigator. You must have an idea? I bet he tells you everything. Mummy says he is sure to have told you.'

John looked stubborn. 'My father says it's a question of morale. That's why it's under wraps. He told me it has to be confidential.'

'So you do know. How close is close?'

He hesitated and avoided her eyes. 'Four point six light years,' he said suddenly.

Tara frowned, considered, and said, 'Yes, but that's the distance. How long is that in travel time? How long will it take us to actually get there?'

'Why do you want to know?'

'Tell me.'

'Why?'

'I need to know.'

John glanced round but the Bodleian Library was still empty. 'If the port engine doesn't get any worse, forty-six years.' His voice was flat, unemotional. He didn't need to look at her to know this was bad news. The worst.

There was another of the silences, longer this time, and when he did look at her, he could see tears.

She spoke softly. 'John? We won't get there until… I'm sixty-two years old! I'll be old! Ancient! We'll be stuck in this ship all our lives. Oh, John!' Her voice had been rising in a wail.

She suddenly looked round the shabby compartment as though seeing it for the first time in the dim light. So dim that they had not needed to switch off the one remaining working light bulb to see out.

'First you complain how funny it'll be on the outside of a planet and now you complain about being stuck inside the old ship.' His voice was fierce, defensive, as though she were blaming him for the laws of physics.

'Old is right. Everything is falling to bits. Look at this room.' She stared round in distaste at the chipped paintwork, the discoloured windows and the all-pervasive dust coating every surface. She looked down at her dress and consciously moved as though to conceal the worst of the mends in the worn hand-me-down.

'Nobody comes here any more. Of course the room is uncared- for,' John pointed out.

'Maybe not, but everywhere in the ship is just as bad. And where are all the people?'

'What?'

'When they started from Earth there must have been loads more people to use all the space in the ship. If it was called "The City of Oxford", there must have been oodles of people in it. I walk down the Cornmarket shopping corridor and feel lonely. The Indoor Market is closed for good.'

'We're not supposed to talk about that sort of stuff. Bad for morale.'

'There are a lot of empty rooms but children are rationed.'

He looked uncomfortable. She was forcing him into forbidden territory. 'Father says it's not the space. It is the food they eat that is the... umm... limiting factor.'

'And they can't even mend our toaster. First they patched it up. Then they patched the patches. Now even the patches don't work. And talking of patches...' She looked down again at her dress.

He found it safer to keep quiet.

She was not to be stopped. 'Is that what's wrong with the port engine? I know it's been patched again and again.' Her voice was shrill with her presumption.

'I'm not supposed to talk about it. Nobody is. Crew morale. Father says...'

'Don't be silly. Everyone knows about it. But nobody will say how bad it is. Go down Broad Street, about a mile down past Christchurch College meadow recreation space, and put your ear to the bulkhead. You can hear it spluttering and wailing. Everybody knows.' She smiled suddenly. 'Mummy says it's all my fault. That I caused it. She says the minute I was born the engine started running rough and it has been getting worse ever since.'

John sighed. 'You don't need to worry. My Father says it will get us down into a good solar orbit, and then they can switch it off for a thorough overhaul.'

'I'm not an engineer...'

'True!'

'...Shut up. But if the engine spares situation is as bad as my toaster...'

'There is a slight difference in priority...'

'...Shut up. And everyone has been economising on power to save fuel for at least ten years that I can remember...'

'...Just a temporary situation that...'

'Nonsense! Just how exactly is this old ship going to haul itself along for nearly another half century?'

'We can make it. We've got to make it. There's no alternative. They've been having meetings about it. Just in case we are out of luck here. We can't return to Earth. It's too far now. Nobody expected the ship to have to try so many star systems. My Father says it our duty to keep going. He knows what he's talking about. I trust him!' John finished with his voice rising defiantly.

'With no certainty of planets at the end? Well! At least I know where we stand now.'

John studied her face in puzzled fashion. 'But I thought the whole point was that we don't know where we stand. We know nothing yet about these planets except they exist. We just have to hope. If we are out of luck there is no alternative to keeping on going. What else is there?'

Tara stared hard through the discoloured plastic at the very bright yellow star that was now nearly a shape and not just a point of light. In the background, never out of mind, was the low moaning of the port engine.

'We do know, though. We do know where we stand. We have to make the best of the planets we can see. We can't go on and on with the ship dying around us. No matter what their faults we have to take what we are given and make the best of it. Star light, star bright!

'And I know this is a lucky star. Sun! It will be our lucky Sun. It will have a planet where we can build domes and bell towers and colleges like in the old videos of Oxford long ago on Earth and we can walk about with no decks above us and it will be very, very scary and it'll have lions and tigers and wind and hurricanes. There will be rain, and I shall carry an umbrella. Yes, a red umbrella.'

She smiled at John and took his hand and kissed it.

'Planets are even bigger than this ship. There will be lots of rooms and corridors.'

John kissed her back in mingled hope and fear, wishing he knew less about the surrounding cold, uncaring Universe as she continued talking.

'And there'll be no need for rationing of children.'

ABOUT THE AUTHORS

Rosie Orr lives in Oxford. Since winning the South Bank Show Poetry Competition she has had work published in several magazines and anthologies, including a PEN anthology and *The Virago Book of Love Poetry*. She is currently working on a novel.

Linora Lawrence has worked at the Bodleian Library and Oxford University Press, and is now at Trinity College. She continues to write for the Oxford Times and their magazine, Limited Edition, and, between all that, works on her own stories and novel. She thinks Oxford still has a wealth of secrets and tales yet to be revealed and feels it is her task to tell at least some of them.

Mary Cavanagh is an Oxford native, brought up in North Oxford. Her first novel, *The Crowded Bed*, was published by Transita in January 2007. Her second, *The Priest's Tale*, is due out this year. She is a past winner of two short story competitions run by The Oxford Times and BBC Oxford/OUDCE. Currently she is working on her third novel.

Margaret Pelling took half a lifetime to remember that her first love was making up stories. Along the way there was research astrophysics, then the Civil Service, and then one day 'Yes, Minister,' became 'Goodbye, Minister.' Her first published novel is *Work For Four Hands* (Starborn Books), and she is now looking for a publisher for the next book, *Capella in Auriga,* while working on a third. Her short story *The Rothko Room* came out in Mslexia magazine.

Sheila Costello has had two children's novels published by Oxford University Press, *The Cats-Eye Lighters* and *The Box That Joanne Found*. She is currently involved with the Oxford-based 13th Theatre Company.

Jane Stemp published two novels for teenagers, *Waterbound* and *Secret Songs*, with Hodder, in such spare time as she had while working as a librarian for the University of Oxford. She is now a rare books librarian for the Royal Navy, and despite an 80-mile weekly commute somehow finds herself with just enough time to work on three more novels at once.

Chris Blount has enjoyed writing throughout his life, making time as a family man and during his career as an investment manager to participate in writers' groups. He had hoped to invest more energy in this hobby after early retirement, but running his own business has certainly foiled that dream.

Gina Claye is a writer and storyteller. Her children's poems have been published in anthologies by Scholastic and Oxford University Press. Her book, *Don't Let Them Tell You How To Grieve* (OxPens), is used by Cruse Bereavement Care to help those who are grieving. She gives talks on bereavement to the Hospice Movement, Cruse and other similar organizations, and can be contacted at gina.claye@hotmail.com

Jane Gordon-Cumming has written stories for magazines such as Woman's Own and Bella, and had short humorous pieces broadcast on Radio 4. Her romantic comedy, *A Proper Family Christmas*, was published by Transita in 2005.

Charles Jones has enjoyed a lifelong passion for writing which has seen dozens of articles and several books published. But he has also filled an old trunk with yellowing paper. All his published works have been non-fiction but he is now working on a sequence of historic fictions set around the turn of the first millennium.

Angela Cecil-Reid spends her days teaching dyslexic children, shepherding her rare breed Cotswold sheep on her farm just outside Oxford, and writing. Her short story *Arthur's Boy* was commended in the Sid Chaplin Short Story Competition while the opening chapters of her current novel for children, *The Dream Cat*, reached the regional shortlist in Waterstone's Wow Factor Competition.

Laura King is an Oxford-based performance poet and award-winning blogger, whose story *The Rising Price of Property* can be found in *The Sixpenny Debt*. For more of Laura's writings, or to book her for a reading, visit http://thepoetlaura-eate.blogspot.com

Gillian Rathbone's literary output includes lexicography (the Oxford English Dictionary), the compiling of a dictionary for learners (Macmillan's), history and nature articles (the Oxford Times magazine 'Limited Edition') and the winning of several short story competitions. Her collection of poetry, *Bus Stop Poems,* was published in 2004 (Whitehill Publishing), with her general collection of poetry soon to follow. She was shortlisted for The Frogmore Poetry Prize 2007 with her poem, *The Lovers.*

Ray Peirson is a prolific and wide-ranging author who has written several full-length novels in various genres – crime, political thrillers, science fiction and also novels for older children – and after an extremely varied career is now writing full-time for publication. He can be contacted at raymondpeirson@btinternet.com

Special thanks to Rachael Claye for help with editing the stories, and to Chas Jones for his advice and support.

Printed in the United Kingdom
by Lightning Source UK Ltd.
135096UK00001B/187-252/P